Always

HOPE

HEIDI RENEE MASON

Dedication

Always Hope is dedicated to anyone who has suffered with anxiety. You're not alone. It is also dedicated to those who have made the long journey to repair a broken relationship. As always, it is dedicated to my husband and daughters— you are my inspiration.

Always
Hope

Chapter One

When I was twelve years old, my best friend and I went to the Ocean Beach County Fair. Rides didn't interest me, but I loved people watching. After a lot of coaxing, Kelsey convinced me to ride the Cyclone. I'd never heard of the ride, and I had no idea what was in store for me, but I trusted Kelsey implicitly. If she said I would like it, maybe I would.

Hesitantly, I allowed myself to be dragged into the line. My churning stomach threatened to expel the funnel cake I'd just eaten, but I climbed on the ride anyway. Only then did I notice that it consisted of nothing but an open, cylindrical space. There were no seats, no handles, nothing at all to prevent us from being propelled into space.

By then, it was too late to change my mind. The door closed and the ride started. Before long, it began to spin, faster and faster, until it was turning so quickly I could barely see. My body was glued to the wall by sheer velocity, and I closed my eyes as I spun out of control. When it came to a halt, my feet met the ground and the world stopped revolving. Kelsey looked at me expectantly, and a huge smile erupted on my face. She was right; I loved it.

We exited through the gate, but all I could think about was riding it again. Giggling, we jumped right back in line and got on the ride a second time. The Cyclone started rotating, turning us around and around inside the enclosed space. My head was suctioned to the side of the ride, but this time, Kelsey told me to look down. Trusting her, I peeled my head away from the wall and stole a glance.

My body was stuck to the wall, but to my horror, I realized that the floor had vanished from beneath my feet. The only thing holding me in place was the force of the spinning ride. I didn't enjoy it at all the second time around; I was terrified. It was amazing the perspective I got when my eyes were open.

I hadn't thought of the Cyclone in years, but two weeks ago, the image of the out-of-control ride popped into my head on the day my marriage ended. It struck me as ironic that I'd been spinning with my eyes closed for as long as I could remember, completely oblivious to everything except the motion of my life. When I opened my eyes, I was shocked to discover that the floor had vanished from beneath me. My safety net of oblivion was gone.

***

Looking out the window of the airplane, I tried to ignore the knots in my stomach. Dark, dismal skies and swirling gray clouds peered back at me, a reflection of my mood. I shifted restlessly in my seat, tapping my fingernails nervously on the tray table in front of me. The walls were closing in on me, and my breathing came fast and short. All I could think about was getting off the plane. The flight attendant, who seemed to sense my agitation, quietly informed me we would begin our descent into Seattle soon.

I nodded slowly at her without making eye contact. It was embarrassing that my inability to cope was so obvious. "You can do this, Hope," I said to myself, taking several deep breaths and trying in vain to settle my nerves. Every muscle in my body was tight, making me a giant, clenched ball of stress that refused to uncoil. I rotated my neck and tried to relax my shoulders. A dull, throbbing ache radiated across my forehead.

The events of my shattered life paraded relentlessly through my head, invading my peace of mind while I attempted to block it all out. I would not think about any of it right now; I couldn't. But try as I might, I couldn't fight off the memories that clawed at my brain like a vulture decimating a carcass.

I pictured my husband on that last day; I remembered the shocked look on his face as I ordered him out of our apartment. It seemed like eons had passed instead of a mere two weeks. His words pounded in my head. It was like a bad movie that played over and over in my mind.

"Please, Hope, just let me explain." Jonathan reached out to put his hands on me, but I ripped my arm from his grasp and took two giant steps away from him. The thought

of him touching me made bile rise in my throat.

"The time for that is over. There's no possible way to explain what you've done. Now get out." I pointed furiously at the front door while I tried with everything in me not to break down and cry.

"I'll go, but this is not over. We will never be over. We've been together since we were kids, Hope." Jonathan looked imploringly at me before he grabbed his suitcase and stalked out the door, glancing back once before it closed. The sound of the door slamming reverberated through the empty apartment. It wasn't until he was gone that I dissolved in a pool of tears. At least he hadn't seen me break.

I shook my head, willing myself back to the present. If I wanted to stay sane, which was getting more difficult every day, I needed to push those agonizing thoughts out of my head. Again I recited, "You can do this, Hope," like a mantra. Maybe if I said it enough, I would start to believe it. Right now, it didn't feel like I could do anything. It took every ounce of strength I had just to keep breathing. Once upon a time I was competent and capable; those days were ancient history.

Trying to distract myself, I glanced around at my fellow passengers. I wondered if any of them were nervous about our arrival in Seattle. I doubted it. I wondered if any of them were teetering on the edge of a major anxiety attack like I was. Also unlikely. I learned a long time ago that the churning, gnawing feeling in my stomach wasn't something most people understood. I wondered what my life would be like if it weren't there, constantly eating away at me. I couldn't remember a time when I hadn't felt it. The tight knots of stress in my gut were as much a part of me as my brown eyes.

I wanted off the airplane; I wanted to turn around and run in the opposite direction. But for better or worse, I was about to disembark the aircraft at the one place I'd promised myself I would never return. It was ironic that I was right back where I started when I had run away ten years ago. But it couldn't be helped. I was trying to escape Jonathan, but he wasn't the reason I had to go home. There were other reasons, other problems I needed to deal with, and although I wanted nothing more than to ignore them, I knew it wasn't possible.

I'd gone over and over the choices in my mind, and this was the decision I'd made. My options were the equivalent of being put to death by lethal injection or firing squad. Either would do the trick, but one would be fast, while the other would take a little more time. It seemed most things in my life boiled down to choosing the lesser of two evils.

"Welcome to Washington. We are beginning our descent into Seattle. The weather is a mild sixty degrees on this lovely March morning. Skies are gray and you're sure to get a taste of the Emerald City's characteristic rain if you stick around long enough." The pilot's announcement over the loud speaker rose above the excited murmurs of the passengers.

Gathering my belongings, I folded my tray table, placed my seat in the upright position, stowed my belongings under the seat in front of me, and prepared myself for landing, going through the motions as I was instructed. Minutes later, we touched down at SeaTac airport. Although I wished I were anywhere but here, I was glad to be disembarking. I didn't do well in enclosed spaces surrounded by strangers, fearing that every second one of those strangers might attempt to torture me with small talk.

Quickly making my way through the vast sea of people, I beelined straight to baggage claim, hoping my luggage would already be there waiting. I observed other travelers excitedly greeting their loved ones. There were tears, squeals of excitement, laughter, and lots of hugging. I wondered what a welcome like that would feel like. The happiness all around made me even more aware of the fact that I was alone. There was no one to greet me; no one was waiting for my arrival.

I stood in front of the conveyor belt waiting for my suitcase. The crowd pushed in around me. I tried to step away, to put some distance between me and the sea of bodies, but it was no use. There were so many people, all lobbying to be the first to pluck their luggage from the belt. Suddenly, I was pushed from behind, the force causing me to lose my balance. My knees buckled and I toppled to the ground, dropping my purse in the process. The entire contents of my bag scattered like shattered glass all over the airport floor. I scrambled to pick up each item while trying not to be trampled by the masses.

The crowd closed in on me and I was trapped. My breath

came fast and short and my hands shook uncontrollably. I knew the signs all too well. If I didn't get control of my panic, I would be in the throes of an anxiety attack right there on the airport floor.

"Let me help you, miss." A kind, soothing voice cut through the fog in my brain as strong, sturdy hands lifted me off the floor and led me away from the crowd. The stranger's hands supported me while I regained my balance.

My head was spinning, but I tried to slow my breathing and regain control. "Th-thank you…," I stammered to the stranger. He released his steadying grip on me, waded back into the crowd, and crouched to pick up my items, placing them one by one into my purse.

"I'm happy to help." He smiled kindly as he placed the bag into my trembling hands. He was around fifty years old, with graying hair and gentle, soft blue eyes. He had the look of someone who was used to taking care of people.

"I-I need…." I struggled with words, still teetering between panic and normalcy. Glancing helplessly toward the luggage turnstile, I saw my bag in the distance, circling around the conveyor belt.

"Is your bag still there?" I nodded slowly, knowing I should get my own suitcase. It wasn't this stranger's responsibility to take care of me. Nevertheless, I seemed incapable of movement and speech.

"I'll get it for you. Just show me which one." I pointed at my black suitcase, identical to every other black suitcase except for the hot-pink ribbon I'd tied to the handle. Luckily, by this time, most of the crowd had cleared and my suitcase was the only one left.

The kind stranger lifted it from the conveyor belt and placed it at my feet. He smiled again, and I gulped, trying to moisten my throat, which felt like sandpaper. My breathing was steadier, and now that the crowd had dissipated, I felt calmer. The grip of panic finally released.

"Thank you so much. I'm not sure what's wrong with me…," I offered weakly, although I knew exactly what was wrong. I'd dealt with panic attacks most of my life, and they never got easier.

"No thanks necessary miss. You looked a little… lost… and I just wanted to help. I have a daughter about your age." He smiled again and the skin around his eyes crinkled. His smile was easy, and I got the impression it was something he did often.

"I appreciate your kindness more than you know." I smiled back, finally in control of my voice again.

"Well, if you're all right, I'll be on my way." He patted my arm.

"Yes, I'm fine now. Thank you again." I felt like I should offer him something, although I had no idea what.

"Please, don't thank me. Like I said, I have a daughter and I would like to think someone would help her if she needed it. Safe travels, miss." The man nodded to me as he walked away. I followed him with my eyes until he disappeared in the distance.

I wondered about his daughter. I envied her, even though I didn't know her. I pondered what it might be like to have that kind of father; someone a girl could count on for strength and for security. I certainly wouldn't know anything about that.

My father wasn't that sort of man. No, he was a deadbeat who had skipped town when he discovered he was about to have a child. He was certainly not someone who made his daughter feel safe and secure. In fact, I had no idea what he was like; I'd never laid eyes on him. I didn't even know his name.

Grabbing my bag, I headed to the car rental counter. I'd left in such a hurry that I hadn't made a reservation; I hoped there wouldn't be any problems securing a vehicle. I did not need another thing to go wrong. Luckily, the rental process went smoothly, and the gum-chewing customer service representative had me driving away from the airport in a Toyota in mere minutes.

The practical, midsized, economy model was the polar opposite of my own car, which was now thousands of miles away. I missed my shiny, fast blue Mustang, which I'd left behind in New York. As much as I loved the car, Jonathan had bought it for me for our fifth anniversary. I told him he could have it. I didn't want any part of him in my life. I sighed, hoping my soon-to-be ex-husband took better care of my car than he had our marriage.

I merged onto the freeway and took the exit that led me toward the coast. In less than two hours, I would be back in Woodridge. Butterflies flapped wildly in my tummy, and my sweaty hands clenched tightly around the steering wheel. Thoughts of my hometown didn't bring about feelings of happiness and nostalgia. On the contrary, I felt nothing but dread, and I knew the uneasiness wouldn't go away anytime soon.

Beads of perspiration condensed on my forehead and a stream of sweat ran down my neck, despite the fact that it was a comfortable sixty degrees outside. Reaching into my handbag, my fingers found the bottle of anxiety medicine prescribed by my therapist. I'd worried that they may have rolled away when my purse spilled. Not that I intended to take them; I was confident I could handle all of this without medication. My therapist, Dr. Holland, insisted I fill the prescription as a backup plan. Reluctantly, I'd agreed, and I realized that I felt an odd sense of comfort as I gripped the bottle in my hot palm.

When I left Woodridge, Washington, at the tender age of eighteen, I swore I would never go back. I said those exact words to my mother as I jumped into Jonathan's car and drove off toward my future. I was determined to shake the dust of our small town off my feet. I was headed for bigger and better things. Woodridge held nothing but pain; memories I would spend the next ten years trying to outrun. In retrospect, I realized that I had been running away from my pain more than I had been running toward my future with Jonathan. As I approached Woodridge nearly a decade later, I was amazed to discover my long absence had done nothing to heal the hurt.

I finally understood that Jonathan Grey had just been a means to an end. I had loved my husband, but I was more in love with the idea of him. I was in love with his larger-than-life personality and the way he could light up a room. I'd always hoped some of his charisma would rub off on me, but sadly it never had.

I'd wanted a hero, a champion, someone to rescue me. In many ways, Jonathan did all of those things. He saved me from life in Woodridge and showed me a world I didn't know existed. I'd thought Jonathan and I would be happy together, and for ten years, I assumed we were. If I'd learned one thing in life, it was that things were seldom what they appeared to be. Ten years ago, Jonathan had rescued me from Woodridge. This time, I would have to save myself.

Chapter Two

I maneuvered the Toyota along the winding, tree-lined route that brought me closer to Woodridge. As I looked around, I began to notice things I hadn't thought of in years. I marveled at the fact that I hadn't passed another car for at least half a mile. In New York, here was a constant barrage of people at all hours of the day or night. I'd forgotten how nice this kind of solitude could be. Gray clouds swirled above me, threatening to open up. I didn't mind the showers.

The saltiness of the ocean air tickled my nose as it wafted through the car's vents. It amazed me, the way an aroma could bring back a memory. The simple fragrance of the salty air carried with it a lifetime of emotion. The maritime breeze smelled like my childhood, ushering in memories both bitter and sweet. It was almost intoxicating; the smell impaired my judgement, turning me from the sophisticated woman I appeared to be into the uncertain girl I once was. In reality, I knew they were the same; my façade of accomplishment was simply a mask I wore to hide from the rest of the world. I was a strange, mixed-up combination of confidence and uncertainty, always trying to piece the fragments together. I'd never really fit in anywhere; my awkwardness forever caused me to feel like an imposter in my own skin.

The sound of my phone startled me out of my reverie. I pulled over to the side of the road and answered Kelsey's call.

"Sweetie, how are you doing?" Kelsey's voice cut through the silence of the car.

"Well, I'm alive, whatever that means." I sighed.

"How close are you?" She knew how much I didn't want to go home.

"I'm much closer than I'd like to be." My voice quivered.

"I know you don't want to do this, Hope. I know there are things in Woodridge you don't want to face. But it's been ten years, honey. It's time."

"I know, Kel. I just don't want to go back to the place where I made the biggest mistake of my life. You know I'm an expert in avoiding my feelings. There will be no avoiding them there." That was really the crux of the matter.

"This is going to be good for you. Just wait and see. Trust me on this." Kelsey, my oldest and dearest friend in the world, tried to soothe my unraveling nerves.

"We'll see. I should keep driving." I didn't want to talk about any of this.

"Okay, I'll call you tomorrow and check in. Love you," she replied.

"Love you too. Bye, Kel." I hung up the phone and pulled

the car back onto the road.

My pulse quickened when I realized I was only about twenty minutes away from town. With a pounding heart, I tried to calm my nerves, but there was no escaping the fact that I was terrified. I fumbled inside my handbag again for the medication, and for a moment I contemplated taking one.

"Don't be weak, Hope," I scolded myself as I dropped the pills back inside the bag. This situation was perfect for the onset of an attack. I was trying desperately not to allow myself to cross that line. Instead of medication, I attempted to use the visualization technique my therapist had suggested, but the only thing I could visualize was the mess that awaited me in Woodridge.

As I drove through town, I realized immediately that nothing had changed in the ten years I'd been gone. The tiny coastal town looked exactly as I had left it. The cedar-shingled buildings were weathered and worn from the salty mist of the sea. I passed Louise's Breakfast House, the run-down, yellow shack that didn't look like much on the outside, but served the best French toast I'd ever tasted in my life. During the busy season, a line of hungry customers wrapped its way around the block each morning. Since it was only March, the doors were locked and it was dark inside. I continued driving and saw Salvatore's Pizza, a local favorite and one of my frequent haunts when I was a teenager. Salvatore's stayed busy year-round; it was one of the few restaurants that always had a crowd.

I continued to the end of Main Street and took a left onto Cranberry Lane. As I drew closer to my mother's house, my palms began to sweat profusely. I wiped them on my pants in an attempt to dry them. I was just around the block, and I knew there was no turning back. This was the neighborhood that had shaped and formed me. It was the first place I'd experienced love, and the same place I'd learned about its devastating loss.

My sadness at being there again was very real, but so was a strange sense of coming full circle. I pulled into the driveway of my childhood home, and felt like I was in the middle of a dream. Amazingly, it looked exactly the same as it had the day I'd driven away in search of a new life.

"What do you mean you're getting married? You're only eighteen!" my mother shouted as we stood in the driveway.

"Yes, I'm eighteen. That means I can finally do what I want. I can finally get away from you. Just admit it, Mom, you'll be glad to be rid of me. You never wanted me here in the first place," I spat back at her.

"You don't have a clue what you're talking about," my mother said through gritted teeth.

"You've never cared about me. In eighteen years, you've never once said you loved me. You've never held me. All you've ever done is criticize me and push me away. So you've finally won, Mom. You're getting exactly what you've always wanted." I grabbed my bag and started to back away from her.

"If you leave now, don't bother coming back. Ever." My mother's face was as hard as stone.

"Don't worry. Coming back here is the last thing I'll ever do." I pivoted on my heel and jumped into Jonathan's waiting car. He pushed the gas and drove away.

I shook my head, trying to clear the images of the day I'd left home. I gazed at the house in front of me, not quite able to believe I was right back there. The blue-painted shutters were faded, and the cedar-shingled siding was a grayish-brown color, turned that particular hue from exposure to the salt water of the Pacific Ocean. The gigantic wraparound porch called to me, inviting me to sink into the wicker furniture where I'd spent countless hours staring out at the sea. The hammock in which I'd spent many lazy afternoons reading still hung at the edge of the porch.

I'd forgotten how much I loved the house. It wasn't fancy; it was nearly a hundred years old, and it had so much character. It was like a living, breathing being. It welcomed me, opening its arms, assuring me that I could do what needed to be done there. How could I love a house so much when most of what had happened behind its walls was painful? I didn't have the answer, but I loved it just the same.

I put the car in Park but didn't get out. It was like my behind was glued to the driver seat. Fear of what was to come kept me frozen, and I knew I was stalling. I noticed that my mother's vehicle wasn't in the driveway and I was glad. I needed more time to muster up the courage to face her.

I looked to my right and saw the house that Kelsey had lived in when we were growing up. After she graduated and moved to Seattle, her parents sold the house and followed her. Although we only saw each other a couple of times a year, Kelsey remained my closest friend. She was my rock. It didn't matter that Jonathan was her cousin; she'd taken my side when I told her we were getting divorced. The only upside I could find in returning to Woodridge was being geographically closer to Kelsey.

Even though I willed myself not to, my eyes darted to the left, and I saw the house where Samuel Mooney used to live. Long before my marriage to Jonathan, Sam had been my world. In an instant, I was transported back to my teenage years. Tears filled my eyes and I heard Sam's sweet voice whisper in my ear, "I'll love you forever, Hope. It's you and me against the world."

Like a flood, the joy and pain of our relationship came rushing back. How I'd loved him back then; how I loved him still. The feelings went deeper than anything I'd ever experienced. Anyone who believed a teenager couldn't fall in love was mistaken. I was proof that it could happen. I'd given my heart to Sam as a young girl, and he'd been its true owner ever since, regardless of the fact that I'd married Jonathan.

I had no idea what happened to Sam after I left town. No one ever told me, and I didn't ask. A part of me didn't want to know. I had a hard time picturing Sam's life without me in it. At this point, though, I was certainly nothing but a distant memory to him. After all, he had a family of his own. He was a father and a husband—the very reasons we were no longer together.

I tore my gaze away from the house. I wasn't sure who lived there now. Kelsey had told me that Sam's parents had been killed in a car accident a couple of years after we graduated, and I remembered being heartbroken when I heard the news. The last I'd heard, the house had been put up for sale. In my mind, it would always be Sam's house. His parents had always been kind to me, especially after our breakup. They knew how devastated it had left me.

Taking a deep breath, I turned off the car and got out. I stretched my legs from the long drive and walked around to the back of the house. The view was breathtaking. Standing on the back porch, I could see straight to the Pacific Ocean. The dune grasses danced in the breeze, swaying in time to the song of the seagulls soaring above. The gentle waves lapped on the sand, and I knew the tide would come in soon. Growing up here, I had taken for granted that I had a front-row seat to some of the world's most gorgeous scenery. Being here again, I realized how much I'd missed the peacefulness of living beside the ocean. There was a quiet tranquility here that couldn't be found anywhere else in the world.

I wondered if the spare key was still in its old hiding place. Ideally, I wanted to get settled before my mother got home. I grabbed my suitcase from the car and carried it to the front door, lifted the doormat, and smiled when I saw the key. I wondered how many times it had been used since I left; probably never. Mom was not the forgetful type, and the spare key had been put there for my benefit. It was one of the only times I remembered her accommodating me.

I heard the roar of a car engine, and my stomach clenched in all-too-familiar anxiety. I should have been prepared to see her, but I wasn't.

Margaret West got out of her car and looked disapprovingly at me, and I was immediately the scared little girl from my past. I gasped, noticing how ten years had changed her.

She looked smaller. In my mind, my mother was a large, imposing woman, regardless of the fact that she was physically petite. She carried herself in a way that was intimidating to people, most of all me. I was afraid of her, and she knew it. Although she'd never harmed me physically, her sharp tongue and biting words had had the same impact.

At that moment, my mother looked like a stranger to me. Time had not been kind. Her long, dark auburn hair, which had always been her best feature, was now cut short and peppered with gray. Nurses' scrubs hung loosely on her startlingly thin frame. Tired blue eyes sank into the sockets and seemed too small in her weathered and worn face; the contours were distinct beneath skin that was stretched paper-thin. At only forty-six years old, she looked as if she could be my grandmother. The change in her appearance took me by surprise, and the sinking feeling in my stomach told me the situation was worse than I imagined.

For the millionth time since deciding to get on the plane, I questioned my choice. Returning to Woodridge might very well be the thing to send me right over the edge on which I was currently teetering; nevertheless, I'd made the conscious choice to do so. I could have remained in New York during the divorce proceedings. I had money to spare, and all of my professional connections lived in the city. My agent and publisher were both there, and quite honestly, I loved New York. The hum and buzz of the city inspired me. The obvious choice was to stay in the city that had boosted my career. Remaining in New York was my plan—until I got the phone call.

My mother's one and only friend, Helen, had called me last week. I hadn't spoken to her in years, and I honestly had no idea how she got my number. As soon as I heard her voice, though, I knew it was bad news. Helen told me that my mother had been diagnosed with colon cancer. She would need surgery to remove the tumor, followed by rounds of chemotherapy to ensure the disease was eradicated. I'd felt as if the wind was knocked out of me when Helen spoke the words. My life was already torn to pieces; I was barely keeping my head above water. I did not need the responsibility of my mother's care on top of everything else.

I loved my mother because she was my mother. That's what children did. We loved our mothers. We loved them even if they gave us no reason to do so. We loved them because, from the moment we were born, our lives were inextricably intertwined, whether or not we wanted them to be. My mother had raised me with no affection and even less acceptance. No matter what I did, it was never right. I spent most of my childhood doing anything I could to make her love me. It never worked. She was prickly as a cactus, and always kept me at arm's length.

As a little girl, I knew she wasn't like other mothers. When I got hurt, she told me to "shake it off and move on." If I was upset, she reminded me that "life isn't fair." I learned early on that if I was looking for affection, I wouldn't find it with her.

She was a nurse, and she worked hard to keep a roof over our heads and food in our mouths. For those things, I was grateful, but the gratitude ended there. She was impossible to please, and was without a doubt the unhappiest person I'd ever known in my life. I had no idea if she'd always been that way or if my father's abandonment and my existence simply sucked the joy out of her.

Her criticism and stringent rules severed any relationship we might have had when I hit my teenage years. We were nothing but strangers living under the same roof. After graduation, I was more than happy to leave and never look back. I called her on holidays out of a feeling of obligation, but the conversation was strained. All I could do was search for words to fill the silence between us.

When Helen called, I knew it was my duty to go back to Woodridge and care for my mother—even though it was the last place on earth I wanted to be. I tried to console myself with the knowledge that I would be far away from Jonathan, but even that sounded like a desperate attempt to find a silver lining. The truth of the matter was that returning to Woodridge felt like a death sentence.

I'd tried to call my mother to tell her I was coming, but she didn't answer and I didn't leave a message. I anticipated a lukewarm welcome at best, but I was used to her cold treatment. Like every other uncomfortable aspect of my life, I pushed it aside and refused to think about it. Deep inside, I knew I needed to help her, even though she would fight me every step of the way. How had I not known she was this sick? We'd talked briefly last month on her birthday, but of course she hadn't mentioned the fact that she had cancer. It had been barely a three-minute conversation.

I didn't know what to say, so I just stared at her, a hundred emotions warring inside me at once. She didn't speak either, but the angry look on her face said it all. There seemed to be no right words, so I blurted out the only thing that came to mind.

"Hi, Mom."

"What are you doing here, Hope? Why don't you go back to wherever it is you came from?" She slammed her car door angrily and walked in to the house, reminding me once again that the choices I made were always wrong.

Chapter Three

I didn't move. I'd known my mother wouldn't be thrilled to see me, so her icy welcome shouldn't have been a surprise, but I was always amazed at the way the woman could put me in my place like no other human being on earth. For the millionth time in my twenty-eight years of life, I wished my mother and I had a normal relationship.

I couldn't remember a time when things weren't tense and difficult between us. I usually dealt with it by running away, and that's exactly what I wanted to do—get in the rental car and race back to New York. At the same time, I felt an intense responsibility as her daughter. She had no one else.

I pushed down my anger, took a deep breath, grabbed my bag, and walked into the house. She was sick; that much was obvious from her haggard appearance. But I had no idea the extent of her illness. She was nowhere to be found, so I assumed she was in her bedroom, hiding from me. Feeling awkward and out of place, I trudged through the kitchen and up the narrow staircase.

At the top, I turned left and into my old bedroom. Everything was exactly the same as the day I'd left. I was stunned. It was like going back in time. I'd expected her to convert it to a junk room, or a sewing room, anything to erase my memory completely. Instead, it was like a shrine to my youth.

It was immaculately clean, which was no surprise since this was my mom's house. I was certain that even dust particles feared her. I slipped my feet out of my shoes and plunged them into the plush beige carpet. The baby-pink walls were still decorated with my posters. Photographs of Kelsey and me at various stages of our childhood were tacked to the walls and framed throughout the room. It was as if time had stopped. Nothing was moved or changed.

I sat down at the vanity table, on the padded chair with the faded pink rose pattern, and ran my hand across the surface. The familiar wood felt smooth under my fingertips. How many times had I sat there as a teenager, closely inspecting my image in the mirror? At least a thousand. Those days seemed like a speck in my very distant past.

I opened the top drawer, and was greeted by my old hairbrushes and makeup. Mom hadn't thrown anything away. I didn't understand; I'd been so sure she would be happy to be rid of me. I'd envisioned her having a celebratory bonfire and torching any remnants of me. Reality was a bit unsettling.

The thought of her coming in here every week for the last ten years, cleaning and dusting around my personal items, made me feel sad in a way I couldn't describe. What did she feel when she came in my room? Did she miss me, even a little? Was she disappointed in our relationship? I'd never considered that my mom might have a soft side. She was so rigid and distant, even when I was a small child. I felt strangely uncomfortable discovering that she hadn't wiped away my memory after all.

When I glanced in the mirror, the stress of recent weeks was startlingly obvious. I'd always been told I was pretty, but right then I just looked wretched. My chocolate-brown eyes were hollow and lackluster; I had angry, dark circles underneath from stress and lack of sleep. My pale, freckled skin was ghostly white, with no trace of the usual rosiness in my cheeks. Golden-blonde hair that normally cascaded in thick waves down my back, now hung limply around my face. I tried to remember the last time I'd even brushed it.

If I were being honest, I didn't look much better than my sick mother. The impending divorce and the news of my mother's illness had taken its toll on my appearance. Then there was my recent miscarriage, which only my doctor and Jonathan knew about. My body and mind needed time to heal, but I seriously doubted that could happen in this house. I grabbed the bottle of anxiety medication from my purse and considered sliding it into the vanity table drawer next to my childhood mementos. I changed my mind and dropped it back into my purse. I might need the pills after all.

I walked to the window next to my bed, leaned on the white, wrought iron frame, and pushed the lace curtains to the side. My bedroom had the best view of the Pacific Ocean. I'd spent countless hours standing at this window, looking out at the crashing waves, dreaming about my future and the day I would finally break away from this place.

Ironically, I was right back where I started. The future of which I'd dreamed was decimated, and I was left holding remnants and scraps of the life I'd wanted. I'd had so many dreams when I'd left home. I'd envisioned a happy marriage, a couple of kids, and a career as a writer. If it weren't for the fact that my books were a huge success, I would feel like a complete failure.

Sighing, I realized that I couldn't hide out in my bedroom forever. Eventually, I would have to talk to Mom. I figured there was no time like the present, so I boxed up my emotions and put them aside. I'd spent my life compartmentalizing my feelings and I was very good at it—most of the time. I kept every painful, difficult memory inside a little box in my mind, refusing to entertain it unless I wanted to. It was the way I made it through my less-than-ideal childhood, and the only way I knew how to deal with pain. I simply chose not to feel it. Unfortunately, there were many things in Woodridge that I'd never been able to box up.

I looked at my lone bag sitting in the corner and hoped the moving truck with the rest of my belongings would arrive soon. I would have to find a storage unit or something until I figured out what I was going to do with my life. It was all like a bad dream. I glanced at my watch and saw that it was six o'clock in the evening, and my stomach warned me it was time to find some food. The kitchen was my mother's domain, and I was terrified of doing something wrong, so I wasn't about to cook anything. I decided to get a pizza, and went in search of my mother to see if she wanted some. Maybe she would view it as a peace offering.

The door of her bedroom was open, and she was sitting on her bed, staring off into the distance. She hadn't yet changed from her scrubs. In fact, I had the sneaking suspicion that she hadn't moved from that spot since she came inside. I marveled again at how tired and old she looked.

I cleared my throat to get her attention. "Mom, I'm hungry. I thought I would run to Salvatore's and get a pizza. Will you eat some if I go?" I stood there awkwardly, half in and half out of her bedroom.

"I should eat, I suppose. Let me get you some money." My mother rose slowly.

"I don't need money, Mom. I can get it. I'll be back soon." I turned on my heel before she could argue.

Climbing into the safety of the vehicle, I breathed a sigh of relief. This situation was much worse, much more toxic than I'd anticipated, and I felt helpless to fix it. I was not strong enough for this.

I turned the key in the ignition and was about to back out of the driveway when I noticed a beautiful little girl playing at the house next door; the house where Sam used to live. She had long, white-blonde ringlets and looked like a fairy running through the grass. She climbed onto the tire swing that hung from the large, sturdy oak tree in her front yard.

As if sensing my stare, she raised her little hand and gave me a shy wave and a sweet smile. I returned her wave before backing the car out of the driveway. I had the strangest compulsion to stop and talk to her, but I had no idea why.

Chapter Four

I pulled up in front of Salvatore's Pizza and was immediately swept away by a wave of nostalgia. I had been there hundreds of times, and the familiarity was comforting. This was one of my favorite hangouts growing up. Kelsey and I would play arcade games and munch on pizza, laughing and talking without a care in the world. I longed for those days, sadly knowing I would never experience that kind of freedom again. The memories kept coming, playing like a movie in my head.

One chilly, crisp fall evening under the streetlight in front of Salvatore's, Sam had mustered up the courage to hold my hand for the first time. He'd grabbed it, his fingers feeling so good locked with mine, and we had walked all the way home like that. I had been fourteen years old, but the memory was as fresh as if it happened yesterday. The stabbing pain in my heart as I remembered it was just as fresh, too. Time hadn't dulled the intensity of the memory or the emotion.

I couldn't bear to think of Sam, and I told myself to stop, but I didn't know how to remove him from my mind. I hadn't been able to extricate him living thousands of miles away in New York, so how could I possibly do it here? Woodridge and Sam were conjoined in my mind; it was impossible to separate the two.

Everything about this town reminded me of him and the intense, all-consuming love we shared. When I thought of things rationally, it seemed ridiculous that I was still hung up on a boy I'd loved when I was just fourteen. The problem was that nothing about Sam had ever been rational, and that was what I loved most about him.

When I was young, I couldn't imagine my life without Sam in it, but circumstances forced me to do just that. Jonathan had been my lifeline, my parachute. He stopped me from hitting rock bottom. Did I love him? In a lot of ways I did, but I knew my love had conditions. For the entirety of my marriage, I'd tried to give my heart to Jonathan. He had everything else—my loyalty, my trust, and my friendship. Despite my best attempts, I'd known it was useless, and deep down I knew why. I couldn't give my heart to my husband because it belonged to Samuel Mooney, and it had since I was a teenager. The thought of Sam was like a stabbing pain in my chest. When I allowed myself to think of him, I could barely breathe. I could picture him so clearly in my mind, and sometimes I allowed myself time to remember. I remembered how the brush of his hands on my skin made me feel like my feet weren't touching the ground. I remembered the tingling sensation of his lips on mine, the heady rush when we snuck away together, our interlocked bodies hidden by the dune grass. With Sam, it was all passion all the time. We didn't know how to come up for air. I barely recognized the girl I was when we'd been together.

Sam had been the only person who could make me forget myself. When I was with him, all the knots in my stomach disappeared and the anxiety that weighed me down ceased to exist. I'd felt free with him, and I ached to feel that way again. He was intricately interwoven into everything in this town, and the memories of him chased me down like a pack of wolves. Our breakup had left me devastated, especially when I had to live with the knowledge that it was my own fault. I could no longer blame Sam as I once had.

I walked inside Salvatore's, and the smell of oregano, basil, and pizza dough wafted through the air. I approached the large counter to place my order, and waited only a second before Anthony Salvatore himself arrived. Mr. Salvatore had owned the place since I was a child, and I was surprised he was still around. I'd thought he was old when I was a teenager, but he looked exactly the same, and appeared to be in surprisingly good health.

"Hope West, is that you?" Mr. Salvatore squinted through his round glasses at me. His bushy eyebrows rose in surprise.

"It's me, Mr. Salvatore. How are you?" I smiled widely at the old man.

"I never thought you'd come back. I'm sorry about your mother. I heard she was sick."

"Thanks, Mr. Salvatore. That's why I'm here."

"You're a good girl, Hope. You always were a good girl.

You know, I read all your books. My wife scoops them right up as fast as you write them. When she's done, I steal them from her. I know they're love stories, and mostly for women, but I still like them. You've done well for yourself, girl."

"I appreciate it, Mr. Salvatore." I smiled at him, feeling happy for the first time since I had arrived. "I need to order some pizza."

"The usual? Or have your taste buds changed in the last ten years?"

"The usual will be great. Nothing better than your Italian Supreme."

He disappeared into the kitchen to prepare my order. I sat at the small table in front of the counter and waited, tracing my fingers over the graffiti carved into the wood. Years ago, Sam and I had carved our initials somewhere on this table. I searched, but couldn't find them.

A few minutes later, Mr. Salvatore handed me the pizza box. I smiled and practically salivated at the aroma. I couldn't wait to dig in. Tipping him generously, I got in the car and headed home. The prospect of sharing a meal and the remainder of the evening with my mother made me nervous, but I needed to get used to it. This would be the first of many uncomfortable days ahead.

I pulled into the driveway and turned off the car. I scanned the yard next door for the little girl I'd seen earlier, but she wasn't there. I pictured her inside her warm, cozy, cheerful house. It was dark now, and she was probably snuggled up in front of the fireplace in her fuzzy pajamas, listening to her mother read her a book. I hoped her childhood was happier than mine; no little girl deserved the sad upbringing I'd received. I grabbed the pizza box and headed inside.

My mom was in the kitchen, unloading the dishwasher and wiping down the already spotless countertops. She held firmly to the old adage that cleanliness was next to godliness. I imagined God himself would be hard-pressed to find anything wrong with my mother's housekeeping skills. It was impossible to spot even a speck of dirt in her home.

Nothing was out of place here—besides me. I was the one thing she'd never been able to control; the one thing she simply couldn't understand. I set the pizza box on the kitchen counter, and my mother stopped cleaning and glanced up at me. She greeted me with her permanent frown, as if my very existence was a disappointment to her.

"Mr. Salvatore says hello," I began, attempting to break the ice.

"He's a nice man. I haven't been there in a long time. It seems silly to order food when I'm perfectly capable of making my own. Most folks these days are just too lazy to do any work themselves." She looked pointedly at me, obviously insinuating that I was one of those lazy people.

"Well, sometimes it's nice not to have to do the work. Should we eat in the kitchen?" I went to the cupboard and got down two plates and some silverware, ignoring her glare as I carried them to the large kitchen table.

"Yes, that will be fine." She scowled.

The view of the ocean from the kitchen was fantastic. French doors opened from the dining area onto the back porch, and the beach was right there, beckoning you closer.

I'd never fully appreciated the view until now, when I was trying so hard not to look at my mom.

I sat at one end of the table, and she sat at the other. The distance between us was more than just physical, and I had no idea how to bridge the gap. We were going to have to coexist for this arrangement to work. We could either continue to ignore each other, or have a screaming match and get it out in the open. I decided to jump into the current headfirst.

"So, were you planning to tell me you're sick?" I still couldn't quite bring myself to make eye contact with her.

"No. I wasn't." She didn't elaborate, and when I glanced her way I saw that she was doing nothing but pushing the mushrooms around on her plate. No wonder she was skin and bones.

"You should have told me. It was hurtful to hear about it from Helen. You are my mother, after all. You should have told me yourself." My voice was sharper than I intended it to be, but I seemed to have little control over my emotions.

I picked at the pizza in front of me as the knots in my stomach tightened. I probably should have just made small talk, but I couldn't help myself. She always had that effect on me. No matter what I did, it was the wrong thing.

"Hope, my decision had nothing to do with you. It was about me and my own comfort. I don't want or need your pity. You made it clear ten years ago that I mean very little to you." My mom refused to meet my eyes.

I noticed that she hadn't eaten a bite and my anger rose. That was so like her, to take my well-intentioned words and turn them against me. She was an expert at always making me feel like the bad guy.

"Well, Mom, perhaps if you weren't so difficult, I would have been more inclined to stick around." The words just fell out of my mouth. She managed to bring out the very worst in me. I wanted to lash out at her; I wanted to make her feel as badly as I did. I wasn't good enough for her. No matter how hard I tried, I never had been.

"You always were an ungrateful girl. I can see you haven't changed one bit." Finally, she raised her eyes to meet mine. "Where's that fancy husband of yours, anyway?"

"Jonathan and I are getting a divorce. I left him two weeks ago." I had a hard time looking her in the eyes while I spoke the truth about my failed marriage, but I tried anyway.

"I can't say I'm surprised. The two of you thought you were better than the rest of us—so high-and-mighty. Running off to New York together." Her next words pierced my heart. "Why didn't you have children? My guess is that neither of you could think beyond yourselves."

The hits just kept on coming. My hands began to shake and I felt as if I might expel the small amount of pizza I'd already eaten. I thought about the baby I'd never have, and wondered how my mother could be so heartless. Losing my baby was the final nail in the coffin of my decimated life.

Three months ago I'd found out I was pregnant, and while I was shocked, I was also ecstatic. I'd never taken birth control, and after years of not conceiving, I assumed there was something wrong with me. My doctor assured me that I was perfectly healthy, but it still never happened. I came to the conclusion that I would never have children, and I accepted it.

So, when my doctor informed me that the sickness and missed period meant that I was pregnant, I couldn't have been happier. Jonathan seemed happy, too. In typical Jonathan fashion, he came home the next afternoon with an embarrassingly expensive sapphire necklace, since September would be our baby's birth month. Jonathan expressed his love with elaborate gifts, and even though they didn't mean as much to me as they did to him, I'd learned through the years to graciously receive them. I'd dropped the necklace on his side of our bed the day I left New York for good. I'm sure he found it when he moved back in.

When I discovered the pregnancy, I had no idea he was having an affair. After I saw the note, written on a well-worn sheet of pink paper that reeked of cheap perfume by the woman who apparently gave him all the things I didn't, I told Jonathan to leave and never come back. To make matters worse, the woman was one of his students. I'd been exchanged for a starry-eyed college girl who had a crush on her professor.

I'd known my marriage was over, but I still had my baby. I was more than capable of being a single parent if Jonathan wasn't interested in having a family. But a few days later, the awful cramping and bleeding crushed the last of my dreams. My doctor said I'd miscarried, and it was more than likely a result of stress. It was just one more reason to blame Jonathan.

My mom stared at me expectantly, waiting for an answer to her question about why we hadn't had children. I measured my words and tried to hide the wavering of my voice as I spoke. "I had a miscarriage recently, Mom, so it looks like you have nothing to worry about. Being a grandmother isn't something you'll have to endure anytime soon."

My heart was being ripped in half, but I wouldn't give her the satisfaction of knowing her words hurt me. I certainly didn't expect sympathy from her, but I'd forgotten just how cruel she could be. I was on the verge of tears, but I was equally determined not to show weakness. I took a deep breath and willed myself to hold it together.

"Look, I know you aren't happy about me being here. You've made that abundantly clear. News flash... this isn't exactly a vacation for me, either. Like it or not, I'm your daughter, and it's my duty to help you right now. That's what I'm here to do. Nothing more, nothing less. You don't have to like it. I don't." My brown eyes locked on to her blue ones, and for a moment, time stopped.

I could sense her internal struggle; I knew her pride was warring with her reality, and I felt a fleeting moment of sympathy for her. "Why don't you make it easier on both of us and at least try to be civil, Mom?"

"I said before I don't need you. I can take care of myself, just as I've done for as long as I can remember. Stay here if you want, Hope, but don't expect me to ask for your help." Without another word, she picked up her plate, scraped the uneaten pizza into the trash, and then rinsed the plate before placing it in the dishwasher. She exited the room without a glance in my direction, going into her bedroom and slamming the door behind her.

I sat at the table, completely alone, but a lot more relaxed now that she was gone. I ate my pizza, and then helped myself to a second slice. As I chewed, I mulled over the impossible situation in which I found myself. I wanted to leave, but my mom's friend, Helen, was right; my obligation was here. My mom would need my help eventually, even if she didn't want to admit it right now. Hopefully, in time, the house wouldn't feel like such a war zone.

I finished eating, put the leftovers in the refrigerator, and made sure the kitchen was once again spotless before retreating to my bedroom. After changing into my pajamas, I climbed into my childhood bed. I couldn't believe I was there. The last few weeks felt like a bad dream from which I desperately wanted to awaken. Unfortunately, this nightmare was my reality. I held out no hope that tomorrow would be any better.

Chapter Five

My cell phone vibrated at seven o'clock the next morning, waking me from my restless sleep. I groaned, fumbled around, and finally grabbed it off the bedside table. Glancing at the display, I smiled. I should have known it was Kelsey. She was the only person brave enough to call me this early in the morning.

As a stay-at-home mom of four boys under the age of six, she was up before the sun, usually calling me on the verge of child-induced insanity. She loved her boys more than life itself, but they kept her hopping. I loved the stories she told me; how Ethan and Harry put frogs in her bed, or how she found Randall and Oliver on top of the refrigerator eating peanut butter nearly every morning. I envied the happy, domestic life she shared with her husband, Daniel, a defense lawyer. In my opinion, she had it all. It was the sort of life I'd dreamed about sharing with Sam once upon a time.

"Morning, Kel," I mumbled into the phone, trying to

sound more awake than I felt.

"Hey, honey. I waited as long as I could to call, but I've been thinking of you since yesterday. How's it going?" Kelsey's voice was a balm to my very irritated soul.

"How you probably imagine it would be going. You know my mom…." I rolled my eyes and sat up in bed, propping myself on the pillows behind me.

"She's still that bad, huh? I thought she might have mellowed out a little, since she's sick." I heard dishes clinking on the other end of the phone and knew that she was probably doing two million other things while she talked to me. The woman did more before the sun came up than I did all day.

My best friend was a little bundle of energy. Her tiny stature, wild brown curls, and laughing green eyes had won me over in kindergarten. Since the day we met, she was the one person who'd always had my back. I distinctly remember the first day of school. I'd been shy, anxious, and afraid of everyone. When recess rolled around, the rest of the class ran happily onto the playground, gravitating into little groups. I stood next to the building, wringing my hands in fear. I was afraid to be alone, but even more afraid to try and make a friend.

At the age of five, I was already stressed out about life in general. I was just about to burst into tears when a little girl with bouncy brown corkscrew curls asked my name. Something about her sweet face and happy energy put me at ease. She grabbed my hand and told me we were going to be best friends forever. She was right.

When Kelsey and her parents moved into the vacant house next door, it was almost too good to be true. Her parents were the kind I dreamed of having. They seemed to know that my life at home wasn't a happy one, so they took me into the fold and included me in their little family. The time I spent with the Norwoods was the closest thing I had to a normal family life.

Kelsey was my rock and my champion. I honestly didn't know where I would be if it weren't for her. She'd been my surrogate mother, father, and sister. I always went to her for guidance, and even though we'd lived thousands of miles apart for all of our adult lives, our hearts were inseparable. Now that I was back in Washington, we could see each other more often. So far, that was the only benefit I could see in this dreadful situation.

"Hope, are you there?" Kelsey prodded me, bringing me back to the present.

"Sorry, I was daydreaming. To answer your question, my mom has not mellowed out. Being sick has made her worse, if that's even possible. It will be a miracle if we don't kill each other within the first week." I rolled out of bed and stretched as I walked to the window. It was a foggy morning, the mist rolling in from the sea. Cool, foggy mornings at the beach were my favorite.

"Well, you're just going to have to hang tough. You are there to help your mom, so that's what you're going to do. She needs you, and you need her… even though neither of you knows it yet." She spoke gently, knowing those words were not what I wanted to hear.

"My mom has made it perfectly clear that she doesn't need or want me here. As for my needing her, I passed that point years ago." The bitterness in my voice was apparent; I couldn't conceal it if I tried, but there was no reason to. Kelsey knew me better than anyone. "Anyhow, let's change the subject. When are you coming to visit?"

"I'm making plans to do it soon. Everything has to be strategically arranged or the world as I know it will fall apart. I have to line up Daniel's parents to come and stay with the boys for a couple of days while he's at work, map out charts and schedules, fix a year's worth of meals…. It's a major event if I leave town, which is why I never do. Don't worry, though, I'm on it." She laughed at all the details she had to work out before she could get away.

"You better be. I need you here," I responded playfully, but the truth was that I really did need her. I was having serious doubts about my ability to see this through.

"I'll get there just as soon as I possibly can. Gotta go, Hope. Ethan just clogged the toilet with a rubber duck… words I never thought I'd say. I'll talk to you soon. Love you—" Kelsey's voice cut off midsentence.

I hung up the phone, feeling very much alone. I had no idea if my mom was still at home, or if she had already left for the day. Since she'd been wearing scrubs yesterday, I assumed she was still working. She was obviously very sick. I knew she would have to quit work soon. Once she started chemotherapy, she would be too weak to work.

There were so many questions I had about her illness. I didn't even know who her doctor was, or if there was an actual plan of action. The only information I had to go on was what Helen told me when she called—that my mom had cancer. My mom and I needed to talk and sort out the situation, but as usual, I really just wanted to avoid the uncomfortable scenario for as long as possible.

I dug through my suitcase, choosing comfy jeans and an old sweater. From the look of the clouds outside, I knew it would be cold; I'd already decided to begin my day with a walk on the beach. I pulled my long hair into a ponytail, didn't bother with makeup, brushed my teeth in the adjoining bathroom, and wandered downstairs.

There was no sign of Mom. Her purse and keys were gone, and so was her car. If she wasn't at work, she'd simply gotten up early to avoid me. Either way, she wasn't there. I toasted a bagel while I brewed a mug of steaming coffee. After making short work of both, I stepped out the back door into the foggy morning.

The minute I was outside, the smell of the salty air beckoned me to the ocean. Following the trail that led from our backyard to the dune grass, I wound my way toward the roar of the crashing waves. The sound was like a warm, comfortable blanket wrapping around me as I snuggled more deeply inside. How I had missed this! I'd never realized how I ached for the ocean until I was here again. Apparently it was just another thing that I put into my box of feelings.

A random memory that I'd locked away years ago bobbed to the surface. I saw Sam and me walking toward the beach, hand in hand, talking about our future together.

"How many kids will we have?" *I squeezed his hand and*

grinned at him playfully.

"At least a dozen," Sam replied.

"A dozen? When am I going to find time to write books if I have a dozen kids?" I stopped walking and dropped Sam's hand in surprise.

"Okay, maybe not a dozen. We can have as many as you want to. I only said a dozen because I was thinking of all the fun we would have making them." Sam laughed mischievously and drew me close to him, running his fingers through my wind-tangled hair.

"Well, when you put it that way, maybe a dozen is the perfect amount." I stood on my tiptoes and pulled Sam's face to mine, our lips meeting with the spark of fire that was always there when we kissed. I loved him so much; my heart was practically bursting with emotion. I wondered how a body could hold that much passion. "I can't imagine anything I would like better than spending a lifetime with you, Sam."

"It's you and me against the world, Hope. It always will be." Sam's voice drifted away on the breeze.

I shook my head and willed the memories to stop. It was getting harder and harder to forget them when everything around me kept dredging them up from the buried past. I reached the shore and stood looking out at the rolling waves. Mist tickled my face, and I could almost feel my wavy hair begin to frizz, but I didn't care. No one was concerned with how I looked here. There was no one to impress. No one was on the beach besides me. At that moment, I was struck with the realization that I was alone—on the beach, and in my life.

Not only was I alone, I was terribly lonely.

Like a slap in the face, I realized that other than Kelsey, I was truly on my own. Truth be told, I knew I had no one to blame for my loneliness except me. If I hadn't been so careless with Sam all those years ago, my life would have been so different. Emotions came in waves, like ocean swells. Being back home was like popping the champagne cork on my bottled-up feelings. The fog mingled with the salty tears that streamed freely down my cheeks.

I shook my head and willed the memories to stop, but they didn't. I was tired of fighting them, so rather than ignore my feelings as usual, I admitted that the isolation hurt. With that admission, a barrage of suppressed emotions floated to the surface.

As someone who went through life numb, I was startled as I began to feel… everything. I stood on the beach while all of the pain I'd tried to outrun finally caught up to me. I thought of the people who'd hurt me, and rather than put it all neatly into a box, I felt it. I had no idea what I was doing, but it seemed I couldn't stop now that I'd started.

There were so many people in my life who had disappointed me. My mom made it clear that she didn't want me here now, and she never really had. While I wasn't surprised by it, it was more painful than I'd ever admitted. I didn't know who my father was, and the mystery surrounding him had plagued me since I was a child. I'd been abandoned by both of my parents in different ways. My father abandoned me physically, and my mother emotionally. One was just as bad as the other. Neither gave me what I needed, and I was overcome with anger, resentment, and sadness.

Then there was Jonathan. I trusted Jonathan implicitly from the moment I met him. From the beginning, I always believed he loved me. I was still having difficulty wrapping my brain around the fact that I'd been betrayed by the person I'd trusted for better or worse.

I've heard that, in every relationship, one side loves more deeply than the other. Supposedly, it is never a completely even playing field. In our relationship, I knew Jonathan was the one who loved me more. In some ways, maybe I even took advantage of his love for me. I never doubted for a second that it would always be there. He practically worshiped me since the day we met. He used to say, "Hope, I'm so lucky you married me. What did I ever do to deserve you?" I never said things like that to him. It never occurred to me to do so.

When Jonathan Grey walked into my life, I was young and broken, caught in a downward spiral, spinning helplessly into a depression over which I had no control. Our paths crossed over Christmas break during my senior year of high school. I was at an all-time low in my life, and I believed I had nothing left to live for. It was more than teenage angst. I was virtually flirting with a complete mental breakdown. My fragile heart, which had just been shattered into a million tiny pieces by what happened with Sam, needed something to hold on to. I had no idea how to put myself back together, and quite frankly, I'd lost the will to try.

Kelsey was worried about me, and rightly so. She was the only one who noticed the black circles under my eyes from lack of sleep, and the fact that my clothes hung on my frame due to a twenty-pound weight loss. Desperate for an intervention, she begged me to accompany her to a party thrown by one of our friends. After a lot of coaxing, I agreed.

Little did I know that night would be life changing. Kelsey showed up at my house with her cousin Jonathan, who was visiting for the holidays from New York. He was twenty-three. He was older and sophisticated, and I remember wondering why in the world he was hanging out with us.

Jonathan was on the cusp of taking a teaching position. I'd met him once before, when we were kids, but I hadn't seen him in years. He was handsome, with black hair and jade-green eyes. He was like a magnet, charismatic, and I knew he could have had any girl he wanted. That night, for a reason I never understood, he made it clear that he wanted me.

I was reluctant at first to even talk to him. I was shy and awkward, certain that once I opened my mouth he would know I was nothing but a silly, unsophisticated girl. He didn't notice any of those things. At the party that night, he never left my side. He seemed to know that I was fragile, and he made it his mission to make me smile. Before long, he coaxed me out of my shell and we talked the night away like old friends.

After Jonathan went back to New York that winter, we stayed in touch, talking on the phone at least once a week throughout the remainder of my senior year of high school. His attention was the one thing that finally brought me out of my depression. He wrote me beautiful love letters and poetry, and I knew I was lucky to have a man like Jonathan interested in me. He was quite a catch by anyone's standards.

I certainly didn't love him the way he loved me, and I told him that from the very beginning. Even that didn't dissuade him. I admired his drive and his love of life, and I also enjoyed his company. It wasn't long before I developed feelings for him. It wasn't love. I'd had that with Sam, so I knew the difference.

When Kelsey and I graduated, he traveled all the way from New York to attend the ceremony. At Kelsey's graduation party, I was shocked when Jonathan proposed, but I said yes without hesitation. My wise best friend warned me that I was making the wrong choice; she knew the truth in my heart that I was trying so hard to ignore, but I didn't heed her advice.

The only thing I knew for sure was my ticket out of Woodridge rested firmly in Jonathan's hands. My mom had no idea I was involved with anyone, so she was obviously blindsided when I announced I was getting married. We argued, and like a stubborn eighteen-year-old, I refused to listen.

Jonathan and I left Woodridge together the next day. We were married at City Hall when we arrived in New York. He knew I wasn't in love with him, but he didn't care. He told me he loved me enough for both of us. That worked for me, but as I'd recently found out, Jonathan needed more.

When I found the note from the woman who claimed to love my husband "more than life itself," I couldn't help but feel guilty for not loving him the right way. I was a good wife to him, but he knew he was not the only man in my heart. I think my version of love had been enough for him for a while, but the time came when he needed something else. I was angry at him for not telling me things had changed on his side. I was furious at his betrayal. He'd been a part of my life for so long that his absence left a gaping hole. He may have never been my true love, but he did have my affection, and I'd always been faithful to him.

My husband had been my cheerleader, my friend, and my life companion. He was the father of the baby I'd lost. We would forever be tied by that painful fact. Even though I knew I could no longer be married to him, I missed the comfort and familiarity of him. I missed all the things that might have been.

Standing there on the beach, I was helpless to stop the barrage of emotions swelling up inside of me. The memories meandered down a mental path, oblivious to the fact that I needed them to stop, until they ultimately ended up at the same place they always seemed to—Sam. The most painful memory of all was that my first and only love was now nothing but a ghost that continued to haunt me. I was amazed that I could love another human being so intensely and survive it. I knew without a doubt that breaking up with him was the single worst mistake I'd ever made in my life. The saddest part was that over the years, I'd come to the realization that I was the only one to blame for us not being together. It was something from which I knew I would never recover.

I reached down and picked up a large shell. It was shiny

and smooth, and another memory of Sam bobbed to the surface. I remembered how we used to love walking on the beach together. We would scan the shore in search of treasures while we walked hand in hand. He always let me find the best ones, so I had quite a collection. I understood at that moment that it was pointless to try not to remember him. There wasn't a spot in this town that didn't have a memory of the two of us engraved on it.

My heart ached with heaviness; it weighed a thousand pounds. I felt like there was an albatross around my neck. I'd unlocked all the boxes, and like water from an opened floodgate, the pain of the memories crashed over me. I cried harder than I had in years, sobbing to the point where I was gulping air, unable to breathe. Why did my life have to be so hard? Why couldn't I seem to catch one single break? Standing there on the beach, drowning in my own sadness, I prayed for a life raft, but I knew no one would throw one my way.

The feelings had to stop. One by one, I placed each memory neatly inside the box in my mind and closed the lid. I visualized it happening, and began to calm down. A person could only feel so much. If I didn't stop now, it would be too late. It was time to move on. I wiped my eyes and steadied my ragged breathing, pushing it all back down, deep inside of me where the pain lived. It was the only way.

Turning my back to the ocean, I made my way up the path leading back to the house. I hadn't gone far when I spotted two figures heading my way. As they came closer, I realized it was the little girl from next door. She was walking with an older woman I guessed might be her grandmother. As we passed, they smiled kindly, and I returned a friendly greeting of "hello."

The little girl's eyes met mine, and she waved shyly, looking at me closely as if she saw everything I was trying to hide. They continued toward the beach, but I was struck again with a sense of recognition. It was ridiculous, because I knew I'd never seen the girl before last night. I wasn't normally the kind of woman who took much notice of children, and I had no idea why this one should be any different, but something told me she was. I shook my head in confusion and continued home.

Chapter Six

I opened my e-mail and was embarrassed to find five from my agent, Reena. I hadn't checked my account in two weeks, and I knew she must be confused, since I always answered messages right away. I replied and apologized for my delay, assuring her that I would be turning in a manuscript soon. Even though I'd told her about the divorce and my mother's illness, it was not an excuse to be lazy. Writing was my job. It's what I got paid to do. Reena told me to channel all of my pain into my next book. There was certainly an ample supply.

As I scoured the cupboards for food, I realized they were quite bare. It was uncharacteristic of my mother to have empty cupboards, and I chalked it up to her being sick. Deciding that grocery shopping was one of the many things I had come home to help her with, I grabbed my keys and purse and drove to Maxwell's Grocery.

Pulling into the nearly empty parking lot, I noticed that

Maxwell's hadn't changed at all since I'd last been there. It seemed nothing in Woodridge had. I wandered inside, feeling like a teenager again as I perused the aisles. I didn't know what groceries my mother normally purchased, so I decided to wing it and buy the things I liked to cook. More than likely I would be the one preparing meals once she started treatment.

Placing fresh spinach and asparagus into the cart, I looked up and saw Will Maxwell, the owner of the store, heading in my direction. Tall, well-built, broad shouldered, and strong, he didn't look a day older than the last time I'd seen him. He was a handsome man in his late forties with dark blond hair and eyes that always held a trace of laughter. He was one of the kindest men I'd ever known.

"Hope, is that you?" Will squinted as if he couldn't quite believe he was seeing me.

"Yes, Will, it's me. I just got back into town yesterday." I smiled at him as he pulled me into a warm hug.

"Look at you! You look just like a refined lady now. No more skittish little girl left in you, is there?" He patted me on the shoulder, and his easy personality immediately set me at ease. Everyone in town loved him.

"Well, looks can be deceiving." I wondered what he would think if he knew the basket case I really was on the inside.

"How long are you in town? What are you up to these days?" He maintained eye contact as he asked each question.

"I'm in town... indefinitely...." I trailed off, certainly not in a hurry to delve into my pathetic personal life in the produce section of Maxwell's.

"I'm happy you're back, for however long that ends up being. I'll bet your mom is glad too. How is she doing? I heard a nasty rumor that she's sick, but you know how folks around here talk. I hope it's not true." Will's face showed genuine concern.

"Unfortunately the rumors are true. She is sick, and I've come back to help her. Honestly, I just arrived yesterday, so I don't know what's ahead of us." I shrugged, feeling again like I was on the verge of tears.

"Oh no, I hate to hear that Maggie is sick." I'd never heard anyone call my mother that name, including Will, until that moment. The two of them had grown up in Woodridge, so maybe that's what people used to call her. Somehow, it seemed too sweet and innocent a name for my rigid mother. "Please let me know if you need help with anything."

"Thanks. I'll be sure to do that." I smiled and told him I would see him around as I pushed my cart away to finish shopping.

It was so good to see him. Ever since I was a small child he had been my friend, but then again, Will was everyone's friend. I'd never heard anyone say a bad word about him. He'd taken an interest in my life from the time I was a little girl, never failing to ask how my mother was doing, and never talking down to me as people so often do to children. I'd always liked that about him.

Once when I was around thirteen, I asked my mom if she knew him. She told me they'd graduated together, but didn't elaborate. She also snapped at me that I shouldn't bother him because he was a busy man. I never brought him up again. She didn't like me talking to anyone in town about her, and discouraged relationships in general. The only friend she had was Helen, and sometimes I wondered how she put up with my mother, but they had been close friends since they were kids.

I loaded my groceries into the car and drove back home. Mom's car was parked in the driveway, so I mentally prepared for whatever confrontation awaited me inside. I toted grocery bags into the kitchen and placed them on the counter. My mom, who stood at the kitchen sink drinking a glass of water, just stared at me as I went back outside to get the rest. I smiled as I came into the kitchen with more bags.

"I noticed there weren't many groceries in the pantry, so I decided to do some shopping. I'm making dinner, too. You can just go and relax." My words left little room for argument.

"What do you think—" Mom's voice was tinged with anger, but I cut her off midsentence.

"It's not up for discussion. You need to rest." I set the last grocery bag on the counter and met her icy blue eyes.

She looked at me as if she had no idea how to respond. She wasn't used to me taking charge of a situation. But I'd made a decision that morning at the beach: this was the way I had to handle things. I couldn't cower any longer. I wasn't a child, and I wouldn't allow her to treat me like one. I was normally the girl who would run around the block twice to avoid confrontation, so running headfirst at it made me nervous. Nevertheless, I knew it was the only way to handle my mother.

It was time to stand up for myself. It was past time to stop allowing her to bulldoze right over my feelings. My heart pounded rapidly in my chest and my palms were sweaty. I wiped them on my jeans. Mom wasn't going to go down without a fight, and I knew I was horrible at standing my ground. But I willed myself to stand there, almost daring her to yell at me for buying the groceries and bringing them into her house without her permission. This time I was ready for it.

A full minute passed and neither of us spoke. As I stood in the kitchen trying not to lose my nerve, I felt like this could be a turning point in our relationship. I watched in silence as an array of emotions played in her eyes, and for a second, I felt sorry for her. The tables had turned and I was no longer the spineless little girl she'd always known. I forced myself to look stronger than I felt. She needed to understand that in order for this arrangement to work, things had to change. She had to respect me.

"It was... kind of you to get groceries. I'll go rest now." Mom's lip quivered and I wondered for a minute if she might cry. Her shoulders hunched and she shuffled slowly down the hall to her bedroom and closed the door.

When she was gone, I expelled the breath I'd apparently been holding. That hadn't gone at all as I'd expected. I'd anticipated an argument; I'd planned for one. I expected her to tell me this was her house and I had no right to barge in and tell her what to do. Instead, she retreated.

It was a small victory, but a victory nonetheless. I knew it would take work, but if we had any chance of cohabitating, she had to understand that I was an adult, a woman, not a little girl she could push around. I grabbed a glass of ice water to quench my parched throat, and began to put away the groceries while I contemplated what to make for dinner.

Chapter Seven

Two days later, I sat in the waiting room at the doctor's office chewing my lip nervously. It had taken some coaxing, but I'd finally managed to pry the information out of my mom that she had an appointment today with her oncologist. I told her I was going with her, and made it clear that it was a statement, not a request. Mom sat beside me, staring off into space without a trace of emotion on her face, leaving me to wonder how she felt.

She must be terrified not knowing what was ahead of her or how her body would react to the treatment and surgery. I tried to put myself in her shoes, and when I did, I felt empathy, something I'd never before felt for her. I didn't normally associate anything but anger with my mother, but on impulse, I reached out and grabbed her hand. She flinched and pulled away as if she'd been bitten by a snake. Her eyes met mine questioningly, and I hoped she could see the compassion I felt, rather than the hurt from her rejection.

Awkwardly, she patted my leg and gave me a weak smile. It wasn't an overwhelming display of affection, but I guess we had to start somewhere.

"Margaret West, the doctor will see you now." A stern-faced nurse led us into the office of Dr. Riddles, the only oncologist within driving distance of Woodridge. He was based out of Ocean Beach Hospital, a twenty-mile drive from home. I knew we were lucky he was so close and had agreed to see Mom; otherwise, we would have to drive all the way to Seattle.

The nurse directed us to the leather armchairs facing the large mahogany desk of Dr. Riddles. He was a kind-looking man in his late fifties who shook our hands as we took our seats. As soon as he spoke, I knew I liked him. Instead of delving into medical terminology and talking over our heads, he cut right to the chase.

"Margaret, Hope, I'm sure you have a million questions, and I'm happy to answer every one of them. Let me begin by saying I have every belief that together we can beat this thing. We've caught it in the early stages, which is good. Until I do the surgery, I won't know the full extent of what we are looking at, but from my preliminary diagnosis, I believe we can eradicate the cancer with a combination of surgery and chemotherapy." Dr. Riddles didn't flinch or look away as he delivered the prognosis. He maintained eye contact with both of us, and it set my mind at ease, knowing that Mom was in good hands.

I waited for her to say something, but she seemed incapable of speech. She looked at me, pleading with her eyes, and I knew it was up to me to be her mouthpiece.

"Dr. Riddles, can you please tell us exactly what the plan of action is?" I cleared my throat as I asked the question.

"Of course. First and foremost, we will do surgery to remove the cancerous mass in your mother's colon. I am cautiously optimistic that we've caught this before it has spread to other parts of her body. We need to do this surgery as soon as possible. I have availability for the day after tomorrow. Margaret, you will need to remain in the hospital for about a week after the surgery, just until you've passed the window of time for the highest chance of infection. Once you've regained your strength from the surgery, we will begin chemotherapy. You will continue the chemo biweekly for three months, at which time we will reassess. I've personalized this plan to you and your individual needs." Dr. Riddles spoke kindly to my mom, who appeared to be blinking back tears.

"The day after tomorrow? I'm scheduled to work that day…." Mom looked at me again for help. Instead, Dr. Riddles intervened.

"Margaret, your days of working are on hold for the unforeseeable future. Between the surgery and the chemo treatments, you will be too weak to work. Not to mention, your immune system will be compromised. As a nurse who works around sick people, you'd be highly susceptible to illness. My recommendation is that you put in for a medical leave of absence immediately." Dr. Riddles looked compassionately at my mother.

"I don't think you understand, Doctor. I have to work for

a living, otherwise I have no money. That's the way the world works." My mom's words sounded harsh to my ears, but Dr. Riddles had obviously heard this argument many times in his career, and he appeared to take her anger in stride.

"I do understand, Margaret. Of course, you may do as you wish, but without this surgery and treatment, I have every reason to believe you will not survive this." The doctor's words, purposely blunt, floated in the room. I knew he said them to make an impact on my stubborn mother, and I waited to see if they would penetrate her tough exterior.

To my surprise, instead of arguing further with the doctor, Mom began to cry. I felt helpless. In my twenty-eight years of life, I had never once seen her cry or show any sign of weakness. Sometimes I wondered if she was even human, she was so hard. Her tears unsettled me, but they also let me know that underneath that tough shell lived a woman made of flesh and blood; a woman who was facing a very uncertain future.

Dr. Riddles looked at me, silently prodding me to comfort her. He obviously had no idea that we didn't have that kind of relationship. Not knowing what else to do, I leaned awkwardly toward Mom and put my arms around her.

Instead of pulling away from me like I expected, she gripped my arms desperately, collapsed into them, and sobbed. Stunned by her uncharacteristic reaction, I wrapped her more fully into my embrace and held her while she cried. I felt my heart expand a little bit as I was confronted with the humanity and the frailty of my mom. I realized in that moment that regardless of what she said, she needed me.

Something inside of me shifted, and I found myself trying to understand her in a way I never had before. Yes, I felt sorry for her situation, but it was more than that. A tiny brick in the wall I'd built up against her crumbled, and a little bit of the bitterness in me left. It was nothing earth-shattering, but perhaps it was a tiny tremor that might incite more little quakes in the future.

I vowed to be there for her from that moment on, and not just out of a sense of obligation. I needed to be there for her emotionally as well. She needed a cheerleader, and I was the only one around to do it.

"Mom, please don't worry about the money; it's not important. I'm going to take care of you now. The only job you need to worry about is getting better." I whispered this in her ear, knowing that she wouldn't want Dr. Riddles to hear me talk about finances.

Mom nodded in understanding as Dr. Riddles handed her some tissues.

"Are you ready to beat this thing, Margaret?" he asked.

She dabbed her eyes in an attempt to regain her composure. I heard the resolve in her voice as she said, "Okay, Doctor, I understand. I'm ready."

We drove home from the doctor's office in silence. Mom looked so tired, and I guessed she was feeling drained, both physically and emotionally. Her surgery was scheduled for the day after tomorrow, and I knew she was nervous about the procedure. We'd had some sort of breakthrough in Dr. Riddles' office, but things were still strained between us, so we didn't speak about what had happened. I didn't know what to say to comfort her, so instead, I said nothing.

We arrived home and Mom neatly hung up her jacket and purse. I followed suit. Glancing at my watch, I saw that it was already five o'clock. I dug through the pantry, trying to decide what to make for dinner.

"What sounds good?" I spoke with fake cheer as I searched.

"I'm not very hungry, Hope. I think I'm going to go lie down. Thank you for driving me to my appointment." Mom smiled weakly at me as she disappeared down the hallway that led to her room. She went inside and shut the door.

Halfheartedly, I prepared some pasta, fixed myself a plate, and stored away the leftovers in case my mother wanted some later. It was a chilly evening, but after the day I'd had, I needed some fresh air. I grabbed my food, shrugged into my jacket, and headed to the porch swing. I sighed in frustration as I shoveled pasta into my mouth.

My heart hurt for my mom and what she was going through. It had been so much easier when I didn't feel anything. Now, I was one large, gaping wound, sore and irritated from being picked at too much. I was no longer comfortably numb to my emotions, and while I knew it was healthier to process them instead of boxing them away, I wasn't used to feeling so many things at once. It was exhausting.

Finishing my dinner, I placed the empty plate on the swing beside me. It was cloudy, and the light was already beginning to disappear. I'd been in Woodridge only a week, but I felt as if I were at least a decade older than when I'd arrived. I longed to feel something besides pain and anxiety;

I wished for peace within myself, but that was something I wasn't sure I could find when I seemed to always be at war with my emotions. The closest I'd ever come to quieting the anxiety was when Sam and I were together. I reminded myself that my life hadn't been all bad. I had my career. I remembered the feeling of accomplishment when I'd sold my first book. In that moment, I knew I was doing what I was meant to do. And even with all our problems, Jonathan and I had some happy times. I'd briefly been able to envision a happy future for us when I'd found out I was pregnant.

One thought of the baby I'd lost, and my lip began to quiver. I'd wanted that pregnancy so badly. No baby would have been loved more than mine. I would have been the kind of mother I'd needed myself. I felt as if any chance for joy was ripped away from me when I miscarried. A surge of anger bubbled like a cauldron inside of me at the unfairness of it all. What had I done wrong? It seemed like Life had some sort of a grudge against me.

Through my tears, I noticed the little girl next door playing. She saw me looking at her and smiled. I waved back and quickly wiped the tears from my face. She appeared to be in deep thought, as if debating what she should do next. Again, I felt strangely drawn to her, and when she looked at me, there was an uncomfortable tugging in my chest. I had no idea what it meant. Maybe it had something to do with the fact that my hormones were still out of control from my miscarriage. My innate maternal instincts were trying to figure out how to handle the fact that I had no baby to mother.

Dropping her jump rope at her feet, she slowly approached the fence that divided our houses. She was just a little bit taller than the top of the fence, and her piercing blue eyes met mine. Her white-blonde hair was pulled away from her face in a ponytail, and freckles danced playfully across the bridge of her nose. She was rail thin and wiry looking, but when she smiled, her entire face lit up like a lightbulb. I smiled back at her.

"Hello, there," I said.

"Hi. What's your name?" she asked quietly.

"I'm Hope. What's yours?"

"Bridget. Did you just move in?"

"This is my mom's house. I lived here when I was a little girl. I just moved back." I didn't elaborate. How could I possibly explain to this little girl what I was doing here?

"I've seen your mom before. She waves to me sometimes." Bridget shrugged as if that explained everything.

"Well, it's nice to meet you. It's always good to know your neighbors." I swallowed as I spoke the words, remembering that Sam used to be my neighbor, but refusing to allow myself to go there right now.

"Bridget, dinnertime," a voice called.

"Gotta go. If she has to call me more than once, I never hear the end of it." The little girl rolled her eyes and took off running toward her house and quickly disappeared inside.

I watched her go, but I couldn't help thinking about what kind of child I might have had.

Chapter Eight

The morning of Mom's surgery, I paced nervously across the blue patterned carpet of Ocean Beach Hospital's waiting room. She had been behind those doors for two hours, and Dr. Riddles had said it could take up to four. I bit my lip as my stomach clenched with familiar anxiety. I knew she was in good hands, and Dr. Riddles had told me it was a simple procedure, but I was still nervous. All surgeries held risk, even the so-called simple ones.

Anything could happen in there, and my mind seemed stuck in worst-case scenario mode. I prayed nothing would happen to her. Things were slowly getting better between us, but we had miles yet to go. I couldn't lose her before we had a chance to see if it was possible to make peace with each other.

Hoping to distract myself, I hopped on the elevator and took it down to the first floor. I'd been there since early that morning and hadn't eaten anything. Mom wasn't allowed to eat before surgery, so I'd abstained from food as well in solidarity. It didn't seem right to shovel food in my mouth when she couldn't. Now, hours later, my stomach was scolding me for neglecting it.

I got in line and chose a blueberry muffin and a large coffee, telling the cashier I'd take it to go. I wanted to get right back upstairs in case someone came looking for me with information, and was just about to jump back on the elevator when I saw Will Maxwell.

"Hello, Will. How are you?" I smiled in greeting.

"Hey there! I'm doing well. How is your mom? I heard she was here today. Word gets around in a small town, you know." His face showed genuine concern.

"She's actually having surgery right now. Snacking distracts me." I shrugged and nodded at my food, trying to avoid eye contact, knowing my emotions were right on the surface. I didn't want to break down in front of Will. That would be embarrassing.

"I'm sure she's going to pull through just fine. Your mom is a strong woman, and she's too stubborn to go anywhere until she's good and ready. And I don't think she's ready yet." He patted my shoulder kindly.

"Thanks, Will. I'm sure you're right." He seemed to have her pegged pretty well. The bell dinged as the elevator door slid open. He and I stepped inside, and I pushed the button for the surgical floor, but he seemed unsure of where he was headed. "Which floor?" I prompted him.

"Uh, the ninth I believe...." His answer sounded more like a question.

I pushed the number nine on the elevator panel. "Is everything okay with you? You're not sick, are you?"

He seemed startled by my question, and I couldn't help but notice that he seemed a bit off. I hoped it was nothing serious.

"No, I'm just fine. I'm here to check in on a friend." His eyes met mine and for a moment, it seemed as if he had something else to say. I waited, but he didn't continue.

The elevator lurched to a stop, the door slid open, and I smiled at him. "This is my floor. I'll see you around."

"Please give my best to your mother." He smiled, but his eyes looked sad, and I wondered if it had something to do with the friend he'd come to check on.

"I'll do that. Take care of yourself." I searched his face for clues, but finding none, left him in the elevator and returned to the waiting area.

I scarfed down the muffin, guzzled the coffee, and checked my phone for e-mails. I returned one from Reena, assuring her that I was hard at work on my manuscript, even though she'd probably see right through my lie. The truth was I hadn't written a word since the day I'd miscarried. Part of me wondered if I would ever be able to write again.

Something in my soul died that day, the piece of me that had still believed in the happy endings I wrote about. If I didn't believe in love anymore, how could I write a book about it? I felt as if I'd been fundamentally changed. Writing books was my job, but I couldn't bring myself to begin something new; I questioned whether I'd ever feel inspired to create again.

"Hope Grey, is there a Hope Grey here?" A round, short nurse scanned the waiting room as she called my name. I cringed when I heard her refer to me as Hope Grey. Having my name changed back to Hope West was at the top of my to-do list. I wanted no part of that woman anymore.

"I'm Hope. Do you have information about my mom?" I tried to keep the anxiety out of my voice, but failed miserably.

"She's out of surgery, and we've moved her to post-op. She should be awake in a few minutes, and once she's feeling up to it, you can go back and see her." The nurse smiled kindly at me.

I breathed a sigh of relief. "Did everything go okay? Did he remove the tumor? Did the cancer spread?" I rattled off question after question until the nurse finally put up her hand, signaling me to stop talking.

"Ms. Grey, the doctor will answer all of your questions when he meets with you and your mother. I'm sorry to say I don't have the answers. I'll come and get you when your mother is awake and ready for visitors." The nurse nodded at me and disappeared down the hallway.

Collapsing into the nearest chair, I cried tears of relief. I hadn't known until that moment how worried I'd been that Mom might not pull through the surgery. I took some deep, cleansing breaths and tried to compose myself, not wanting to be a teary-eyed mess when I went back to see her. I remembered that I'd promised to let Helen know when Mom was out of surgery; she would be worried about her friend.

"Hope?" Helen picked up on the first ring.

"Yes, Helen. She's out of surgery. They said it went well."

I smiled to myself.

"That's great news. I've been so worried. Thank you for letting me know. Give Margaret a hug for me and tell her I'll swing by to see her tomorrow," she replied.

"I will," I promised.

"And Hope? Thank you for being with her. I know things are rough between the two of you, but I promise you, you're just what she needs." She thanked me again and hung up.

A few minutes later, they led me into the post-op room where Mom appeared to be sleeping. Her lack of motion took me by surprise, since I thought they were waiting until she was awake to bring me back. As I got closer to her bed, though, I realized she was awake, just very still.

She looked so small and frail in the bed, and I was momentarily shocked at seeing her so vulnerable. It was jarring and unsettling. Mom was fierce, sharp-tongued, and strong; but right now she just looked old, tired, and very sick. I swallowed the lump that rose in my throat and pushed back the tears that filled my eyes. I had to be strong enough for both of us.

"Hey, Mom." I reached out tentatively and touched her arm. We were both still uncomfortable with overt displays of affection, but I felt as if I needed some kind of connection with her, even a small one.

"Hope…" Her voice sounded raspy, but she reached up and squeezed my hand. I prayed the surprise I felt didn't show on my face when her hand grasped mine. It was the only time I remember her reaching out to me physically. Her small, bony hand felt foreign as I gripped it in my own.

"The nurses say you did great in surgery. Dr. Riddles will be in soon to talk to us, but I'm sure he's going to tell us good things, too." I tried to sound encouraging, and hoped I was right.

"Hope, I… I'm sorry…." Mom had tears in her eyes and appeared to be apologizing for something, but I wasn't sure what. She was having trouble getting the words out.

"Sorry for what, Mom?" I asked in confusion.

"For… everything…." Her eyes met mine, and for the first time in my life, I really saw my mother. Not the angry, rule-driven, nothing-I-did-was-ever-good-enough mother. I saw the woman she was underneath all of that. The one who'd raised a daughter alone; the woman who'd never had anyone to depend on besides herself. I saw someone facing her own mortality, and I saw the raw, honest fear behind her blue eyes. I also saw guilt and shame, perhaps stemming from all the unhappiness we'd caused each other.

"I know. I'm sorry too." I had no other words to offer, but I decided she might have just needed to be heard.

She smiled at me weakly, then closed her eyes and drifted back to sleep. The nurse had warned me she would be groggy for the rest of the day, so I assumed her drifting off was normal. My heartbeat quickened thinking of the words she'd just said. Strangely, I felt lighter and less burdened than I had a few moments ago. My mom's apology, in spite of the years of pain, freed me in a way I'd never imagined it could.

Honestly, I'd never even realized how much anger I harbored against her for my painful childhood until I felt it release a little bit. I knew it wasn't like waving a magic wand. Truth be told, we still had many hurdles to jump, but it was the start of something new, and for that I was grateful. I hadn't really had a mother all my life, but maybe, as the old saying went, it was better late than never.

About that time, Dr. Riddles came in and caught me wiping tears from my eyes. I'm sure he thought I was crying because I was worried about my mom.

"Hope, your mom is resting comfortably. That's good. I plan to meet with her when she's a little less drowsy, but you've been here since early this morning. You should go home and get some rest. Doctor's orders." Dr. Riddles smiled kindly at me and patted my hand, which still held my mom's.

"Can you give me any information? Please? I will rest much better if I know your opinion about how the surgery went." My eyes pleaded with him.

"Well, the prognosis is good. I'm fairly certain that I was able to remove the entirety of the tumor. As long as no rogue cancer cells managed to escape, I believe we can likely say she is cancer free. However, I still want Margaret to do the chemo rounds. This is a precaution to ensure that we've entirely eradicated the disease from her body, making sure the cells don't travel anywhere else. She'll remain here for at least four days to recover from the surgery, and then in a couple of weeks, when she's stronger, we will begin the treatments." The doctor smiled at me as he delivered the news I'd been praying to hear.

"Thank you, thank you, Dr. Riddles. Thank you for everything." My heart practically danced in my chest at the news. "I think I can rest now. Please tell her I'll be back tomorrow when you talk to her later."

I patted Mom's arm, grabbed my jacket and purse, and made my way to the parking lot to find the car. Climbing inside, I began the short drive home. My brain was racing a million miles an hour. It had been a long, exhausting day, but the outcome was better than I'd allowed myself to imagine. Dr. Riddles believed my mom was cancer free, and after the chemotherapy, he was optimistic that she would be for sure. More miraculous than that, though, was the fact that she had apologized to me. That was something I thought I'd never hear in my lifetime. They said that everything happened for a reason, and I was beginning to believe it was true.

Chapter Nine

Long shadows and the last glimmering rays of sunlight greeted my eyes as they fluttered open. Pulling my brain from its sleep fog, I registered that someone was knocking on the front door. I fumbled around and finally found my cell phone on the coffee table in front of me, blinking twice when I saw that it was six o'clock in the evening.

I jumped off the sofa, where I'd apparently napped away the entire afternoon, and jogged to the front door. I had no idea who was there or how long they'd been knocking. I couldn't believe I'd slept so long. It seemed like I'd just sat down to check my e-mail, but that was three hours ago. Obviously I'd been more tired than I'd realized.

Opening the front door, I was surprised to see Bridget from next door standing beside the older woman I'd seen her with at the beach.

"Hello." I smiled, confused as to why they were there.

"Hi, Hope. This is my Grandma June. I told her about

you, and she wanted to meet you. We brought cookies, too." Bridget smiled and extended a plate of delectable, homemade chocolate chip cookies. My mouth practically watered as I invited them into the kitchen, placing the cookies on the table.

"It's nice to meet you, Hope. Bridget said the two of you made friends, so we decided we would bring you some cookies." June patted me kindly on the shoulder as she smiled. I wasn't usually comfortable around strangers, but she exuded a calming air that immediately put me at ease. She struck me as the kind of woman to whom you could spill your entire life story without even realizing you'd done so.

"Thank you very much. What a thoughtful gesture!" I couldn't believe they had gone out of their way to make something for me, a practical stranger.

"Chocolate chip's my favorite. I hope you like them." Bridget smiled widely and I noticed she had a look of metamorphosis about her, as if she wasn't yet what she would be. She was a bit skinny and gangly, all arms and legs, but I could tell she would be stunning when she grew into herself. She also had a wise, knowing look that seemed to see something in me that I was trying to hide. It was a bit unnerving.

"Your intuition is great, Bridget. Chocolate chip's my favorite too. Would the two of you join me in having one with a cup of tea?" I offered.

"We would love to, Hope, but I have to get Bridget started on her homework. It's a school night, right, Miss Bridget?" June ruffled her granddaughter's hair and I smiled as Bridget rolled her eyes dramatically.

"Sure, Grandma June, homework sounds way better than cookies." Sarcasm practically dripped from the little girl's tongue. It took all of my willpower not to laugh out loud.

"Well, thank you so much. I'm touched by your kindness. Let's get together sometime soon?" I said as I led them to the front door.

"Of course, dear." June smiled at me, and then turned to Bridget. "Darling girl, you run home and get started on your homework."

"All right, Grandma. See you, Hope!" Bridget bid me a reluctant farewell and trudged next door to follow her grandma's instructions.

"Dear, how is your mother?" June turned back to me as soon as Bridget was out of earshot. Her question caught me off guard. I'd had no idea she was acquainted with Mom or her situation. Obviously they were neighbors, but Mom wasn't very social. The surprise must have shown on my face, because June continued by way of explanation. "It's a small town, you know. These things get around."

"Well, she had surgery today, and Dr. Riddles says the prognosis is good. She'll still have to do chemo when she's stronger, though. That's going to be tough for her." I didn't want to say too much, but it was so kind of her to ask about Mom.

"I lost my husband to cancer, Hope, so please, if you need anything, don't hesitate to ask. Sometimes the disease is nearly as hard on those who are the caretakers." June reached out and patted my shoulder again, and I had the sudden longing to be cradled in this woman's maternal arms. It was the strangest sensation. I was obviously an emotional basket case.

Rather than embarrass both of us by throwing myself at her, I blinked back the tears that were threatening to spill over. "Thank you. That means a lot to me. And thank you for the cookies."

"You're welcome, dear. We will see each other soon." She smiled again before she turned and headed home.

I walked back inside, still surprised at the kindness of my neighbors. I'd lived in New York for ten years and had no idea who my neighbors were. My stomach growled in hunger, and I realized I hadn't eaten since the hospital. I glanced at the plate of cookies on the table. I could do one of two things: I could make a nutritious dinner, or I could singlehandedly devour the cookies. The decision was obvious. I removed the plastic wrap and took a bite of the first cookie. It was gooey, soft, and still warm. Basically, it was heaven on a plate. I made quick work of the first one and was about to move greedily onto the next when I heard my phone ringing.

Grabbing it off the coffee table, I answered without glancing at the display. As soon as I heard his voice, I kicked myself for not screening the call. It was Jonathan, the last person on earth with whom I wanted to have a conversation.

"Hope, don't hang up," Jonathan, who knew me too well, said quickly.

"What do you want?" I asked testily.

"To talk. Just to talk." His voice, as well known to me as

my own, sounded like everything safe and comfortable.

I wanted nothing more than to collapse into his familiarity after the stressful day I'd had. The temptation to unburden myself to the man with whom I'd shared a large portion of my life was strong. He had a way of making problems seem more bearable, and that was one of the things I missed about him. I reminded myself that I couldn't do it; he was no longer that person to me.

"We have nothing to say to each other, Jonathan." I steeled myself to deliver the words that needed to be said.

"Fine. Don't say anything then. Just listen." His voice was pleading.

"Nothing you say will change what happened. It's over."

"Babe, I screwed up, big-time. But I miss you. I need you back. I'll spend the rest of my life making it up to you."

"No! If I can't trust you, there's nothing left for us."

"Please don't say that! We've been together since we were kids. It can't be over. It won't ever be over."

"Good-bye, Jonathan." I clicked End on my phone before he could say another word, because I knew that he might persuade me if he kept talking.

Fresh tears started to fall; it seemed that crying was all I could do lately. I curled up on the sofa and let them come. It was just me now; I didn't have to be strong. If I were being honest with myself, I did miss Jonathan. He was right, we'd spent so much of our lives together, and he was the only family I'd had for years. Would it really be so bad to forgive him? Maybe we could go to counseling and start over? I knew other couples who'd successfully done that.

But even as the thought began to form in my brain, I knew it wasn't ever going to happen. To me, honesty was everything. If I couldn't trust him, I couldn't be married to him. I would always be wondering where he was and who he was with. My suspicion would drive me crazy. No amount of counseling would change that.

I knew I hadn't been a perfect wife, but the one thing I'd always been was honest. I deserved the same courtesy. I knew with certainty that my marriage was over, and as much as it pained me to admit it, this was the first thing I'd been sure about in a really long time.

Despite the fact that I'd spent the entire afternoon sleeping, I was exhausted. I knew my fatigue wasn't really physical; I was emotionally drained. I felt as if my heart had been plowed over by a bulldozer, so I locked up the house and headed upstairs. The problem was, I didn't want to sleep; I honestly had no idea what I wanted. I was tired, but restless, so I went into my bedroom and flopped onto my childhood bed in exasperation. My life was officially a big, complicated mess.

Looking out the large window next to my bed, I saw that it was a rare, clear night. It was so clear that I could actually see the stars, and suddenly, I knew exactly what I needed; I needed a moment of clarity. Grabbing my sweater and a fluffy blanket, I unlocked the window. It creaked and groaned as I pushed it open and removed the screen. I poked my head outside and looked down. My stomach flipped when I saw that the ground was a great distance away. It was much farther away than I remembered.

"Don't be a baby, Hope. You used to do this all the time." I gave myself a pep talk as I carefully eased my body out the window and onto the roof. My legs were actually shaking as I attempted to secure my footing on the sloped roof. Almost-thirty-year-old women did not climb out windows onto roofs. I was too old for this, and would most certainly lose my footing and plummet to my death. Obviously, I'd been much braver as a teenager, because I never thought twice about it then. What was I thinking? This was quite possibly the worst idea I'd ever had.

With a death grip on the side of the house to keep me stable, I slowly lowered myself to a sitting position. My heart was running laps inside my chest, and I willed it to slow down. I wrapped the blanket around my shoulders, hoping to stop the chattering of my teeth. Honestly, I wasn't sure if they were chattering from the cold or from absolute fear.

Once I was situated, I looked around and the old familiar feeling began to replace the fear. I used to come out here nearly every night, rain or shine, when I was a teenager. It was the one place where I felt like I could truly escape all expectations and just be still. As I glanced at the house next door, I was painstakingly reminded that this was just another thing I'd shared with Sam. This was our nightly meeting place. His bedroom window was across from mine, and we would both climb out and sit on the roofs of our houses.

Most of the time we didn't talk, but we didn't need to. We just shared the moment in easy silence, communicating only with a look. With Sam and me, words weren't always necessary, and as I came to find out, sometimes my need for words did far more damage than silence ever could. There wasn't another human being in the entire world that I'd ever felt as close to as I had Sam, not even Kelsey. I'd never believed in soul mates until I fell in love with him, but if two people were ever meant to be together, I knew it was us.

I was certain, even with everything that happened later, that Sam believed it too. That's why losing him hurt so much. For the last ten years, I'd been haunted by the ghosts of what might have been. Living among those ghosts was painful, knowing every day that you're dying inside, yet not being able to do anything about it.

These days, Sam was my past, but at one time, he'd been my future. I felt like I'd always been living in the shadow of that future. My life after him was just a quasi-life, something I existed inside of, but never really lived. It was a far cry from the life we'd planned together. In the recklessness of youth, we'd thrown away any possibility of that life we'd planned in one terrible night. Sam and I were both passionate, and sometimes that fire burned so intensely that we said or did things we didn't mean in the heat of the moment. I was guiltier of that than he was. I remembered distinctly the night it all unraveled.

It was November of our senior year in high school and we had been walking along the beach. Like a careless little girl who had no idea the treasure she held in her hand, I'd started a silly argument with Sam. I'd made a jab about him being interested in one of our classmates, Annie. Everyone in school had known that Annie liked Sam. She made no secret of the fact that she would steal him from me if she could. She'd flirted shamelessly with him, throwing herself at him any time she had the opportunity. He had tried his best to ignore her advances, but she was difficult to ignore. Annie and I had never gotten along. She'd been popular, wild, and a free spirit; she'd been everything I wasn't. At the time, I didn't understand that I was jealous of her in many ways, but the maturity of ten years had given me some perspective on that. I had since realized that I'd felt threatened by her, worried that Sam might want a girl like Annie. Most of the guys in school had.

Earlier that day, Annie's friend had told me that she'd seen Annie and Sam in the hallway together, making plans with each other to meet up later that night. I should have known that it was meant to get under my skin; I should have taken it for what it was. Instead, I began to doubt Sam's loyalty to me. Had they made plans to meet? Was he interested in her? For the rest of the day, jealousy and insecurity ate at me. It wouldn't let up. That night, as we'd walked along the beach, I'd unleashed it on Sam, accusing him of having a thing for her. Deep inside, I'd known it wasn't true, but for some reason, I'd said it anyway. Of course, he denied that he was interested in her, and tried to calm my rage, but I was unrelenting. The more he'd denied it, the more I'd accused him. I'd allowed the rumors to get under my skin and chip away at the only thing I'd ever been sure of—Sam's love for me. I'd yelled things at him, hateful things that could never be taken back.

"I hate you, Sam! I never want to see you again!" I'd

screamed through my sobs. It couldn't have been further from the truth, but I'd flung the words at him anyway.

In all of our arguments, I'd never said that before, and I could tell from the look on his face that I'd broken his heart. I was not in control of my emotions that night, and nothing he said would change my mind. Determined to hold my ground, I walked home and refused to answer his calls. I stewed in my own self-righteousness for a while, certain that I'd done nothing wrong. But the more I thought about it, the more I understood that Annie and her friend had played me for a fool. I did the exact thing she wanted me to do—break up with Sam.

As I began to understand that, my rage and indignation turned into shame and regret, but I was still too stubborn to back down. For the next few days, I'd avoided all the places that I might run into Sam; I didn't go on the roof at all. I knew he was there. I saw him sitting outside each night, silently pleading with me to talk to him. Instead of giving in, I'd rudely closed the blinds so I wouldn't see him sitting there. Inside, my heart was breaking. I'd wanted to fix the damage I'd caused, but I didn't know how. So instead, I masked the confusion with anger.

My irrational feelings lasted for over two weeks. I finally came to my senses and decided to beg him to forgive me and forget it. He loved me and I loved him, and that was all that really mattered. I had been certain I could make things just fine again. But my own fear and embarrassment got in the way, and it took me another six weeks before I finally worked up the nerve to face him.

I'd never forget the day I walked to his house and rang his doorbell; it was a day that would be forever etched into my brain. I'd smiled apologetically when he'd answered the door, praying that he would see the contrition on my face and know that I still loved him and was so sorry for everything I'd said to him. As soon as I saw his face, I knew that he'd been crying. I reached out for his hand, but instead of grabbing mine, he pulled away as if it were on fire.

"I'm sorry for what I said, Sam. It was stupid of me to accuse you of wanting to be with Annie. I know you love me, and I love you. Is there any way you can forgive me?" I remembered how my voice quivered with fear and nervousness.

I'd begged him to take me back, throwing away every ounce of pride that I still had. Nothing I said made one bit of difference. I'd been so sure when I knocked on his door that I could easily fix the situation I'd created, but when his face crumpled and the tears began to spill, I knew that was impossible.

My entire world changed that afternoon on his porch. Instead of winning back the love of my life, I realized I'd lost him forever. For many years I tried to blame him for what happened. I convinced myself for a while that his actions had destroyed everything. As I thought about it that night on the roof, though, I admitted for the first time that I was the only one to blame. I'd accused Sam of something he'd never done. I'd told him I never wanted to see him again. I'd been the one who'd crushed our dreams of a future together. In a moment of weakness and anger at me, Sam went straight to the girl I'd accused him of wanting. He and Annie had a one-night stand, and that mistake would change all our lives forever.

I would never get to make things right with Sam. In fact, I never spoke to him again after that day. I remember my heart being ripped in two as he told me it was impossible for us to be together; he and Annie were getting married after graduation. He felt it was best to make a family for the baby they'd created the night I broke up with him.

Chapter Ten

After my gut-wrenching walk down memory lane last night on the roof, I'd cried myself to sleep. I woke up feeling positively drained, but I knew I had to shake it off and go visit Mom, so I got ready quickly and headed out. My first stop was coffee. It was early in the day, but I was already tired. I pulled away from the coffee stand, thanked the barista, threw a tip in the jar, and steered Mom's car onto the winding road that led to Ocean Beach Hospital. I'd returned the rental car last week, and I knew that I would need to buy my own eventually. For the time being, though, I was using Mom's. I yawned, took a sip of the black magic, and willed the caffeine to speed through my veins quickly. Mom would be more alert today, and I wondered if she would remember our breakthrough conversation yesterday, or if she'd been too medicated to be aware of what she'd said.

Part of me hoped she would remember. Her apology was a big step on our road to reconciliation. I wanted to keep going forward, not in reverse. I glanced at the bouquet of flowers I'd picked up at the flower shop this morning and smiled. They were gerbera daisies, Mom's favorite flower. I remembered her telling me once when I was a little girl that they were the happiest flowers, and I'd wondered why a perpetually unhappy woman would care about happy flowers. They had caught my eye this morning, and I hoped they would bring a little joy into her hospital room.

I pulled into the parking lot, locked up the car, and headed to the fifth floor. Dr. Riddles had left a message this morning letting me know that he'd already made his rounds for the day, so I wouldn't see him. He relayed that Mom was doing well and had been moved into a permanent room on the fifth floor.

This was good news, and I tried to pull myself out from under the cloud of gloom that seemed to be following me. Letting myself remember too much last night had been a bad idea. Going onto the roof, where I was stampeded by memories of Sam, was an even worse idea. I probably shouldn't do it again, but deep down, I knew I would. I was a glutton for punishment these days.

I stepped off the elevator and walked down the hall to Mom's room. Knocking lightly on the half-open door, I heard her say, "Come in."

"Hey, how are you feeling today?" I stood awkwardly next to her bed, not quite sure what to do next.

"Um… I'm sore…." Mom tried to sit up a little more in bed and winced in pain at the effort.

I placed the flowers on her bedside tray and tried to

help her adjust her body in the bed. Once she was settled, I wedged a pillow behind her back to help prop her up a bit. "Better?"

"Yes, thank you." Mom cleared her throat and gave me a shy smile. "The flowers are lovely. They're my favorite."

"I know. I remembered." I shrugged, not sure what else to say.

"One time, when I was seventeen, my boyfriend bought me a huge bouquet of them; every color in the rainbow. My father had an absolute fit. He said I was too young to be getting flowers from a boy, and he threw them out the back door into the yard, vase and all. I was heartbroken. When he and my mother went to sleep that night, I snuck out and got them. I took them up to my room and pressed them between a stack of books to dry. I probably still have them somewhere…." Mom was momentarily lost in the memory, and I noticed that her face took on a softer look.

She'd never revealed any information about her parents before, and I found myself feeling sorry for the young girl she must have been. It sounded to me like perhaps she hadn't had a great family life either; that might explain why she never knew what to do with me.

I was intrigued with the idea of Mom having a boyfriend. She hadn't ever mentioned dating or boyfriends. Obviously, I was aware that she'd had at least one in her lifetime, since I wasn't the Immaculate Conception, but she never talked about her past. I found myself wanting to know more about my mother. I'd honestly never given any thought to her life before me.

"You never mentioned any boyfriends before. What was he like?" I wondered if she would answer or completely shut down.

"Oh, that was a long time ago, Hope. It's not important." Mom waved her hand, as if she were shooing away the old memory. I decided not to push her. Instead, I surprised myself with what I said next.

"So, I've been thinking a lot about when I was younger. I think it might have something to do with the fact that I'm sleeping in my childhood bedroom. I was wondering… did you keep my old high school yearbooks? They used to be on the bookshelf downstairs, but I noticed the bookshelf is gone. It might be fun to take a look at them after all these years." I hadn't intended to ask the question, but it sort of just fell out.

"That old bookshelf was falling apart. I took most of the books to the used bookstore, but I boxed up your yearbooks and put them in the attic. You're welcome to poke around if you want." She took a sip of her water and cleared her throat. Her voice sounded weak, and she looked so tired. I knew she was trying to stay awake and alert since I was there. It was probably best if I went home and let her rest.

"I think I'll do that this afternoon. It might be fun. You look exhausted, Mom. If you want to rest, I can leave…." I didn't want to run off and leave her alone, but I also didn't want her to stay awake to entertain me.

"I'm sorry, but I'm worn out. I don't want to rush you off, but a nap does sound really nice…." She shrugged, and I could tell she was trying very hard not to hurt my feelings.

I was surprised that she cared how I felt. It seemed we really might be forging a new path.

"Please don't apologize. You've been through a lot. The best thing you can do is rest. So, I'm going to go home and let you do just that. I'll check on you tomorrow." I bent down and placed a tentative kiss on her forehead. I had no idea what possessed me to do so. She tensed momentarily, but it only lasted a second before I felt her relax.

When I stood up, I noticed she had tears welling up in her eyes, ready to fall. She patted my hand. "You're a good girl, Hope. I'm sorry I never told you that before. But you are."

I couldn't have been more shocked if my mother told me she'd been abducted by aliens. Who was this woman? Not that I was complaining. It was just all so unexpected.

"Thanks. And you're a good woman. I don't think I've ever told you that before either."

I left the hospital with a very grateful heart.

When I arrived back home I was hungry. After feeding myself, I climbed the stairs to the attic. It was dark and dusty, and to be honest, I was a little creeped out. I felt along the wall for the light switch, and breathed a sigh of relief as the room lit up. I hadn't come up here much as a child, and looking around I remembered why. Dust bunnies lurked in the corners and cobwebs lined the ceiling. In spite of myself, I really was curious about what was hidden up there, so I put on a brave face and started looking.

Meticulous as always, even in the attic, Mom had carefully labeled each and every box and stacked them all in neat rows along the wall. I wouldn't have been a bit surprised if they were alphabetized, too. I found one that was labeled Hope and removed it from the stack. Luckily it was on top, so I didn't have to worry about everything else tumbling over in the process. I opened the lid and was amazed at all of the memorabilia inside. There were old photographs and yearbooks, as well as some school papers I'd written.

I couldn't wait to investigate. I decided to carry it downstairs to my room to inspect the items, since the idea of hanging out in the attic wasn't very appealing. I was about to leave when I noticed a box sitting off to the side, away from all the rest. It wasn't labeled, which seemed strange to me considering the careful organization of the other boxes.

"It's probably nothing important. Just grab your box and get out of this creepy attic." I spoke aloud and the sound of my voice echoed off the walls.

Curiosity got the better of me, and I walked over and carefully opened the lid of the unmarked box. I'm not sure what I expected, but I gasped as I looked inside. It was filled with stacks of letters, and lying on top of them was a bouquet of dried gerbera daisies.

I knew the letters weren't mine, and it was an invasion of privacy to look at them, but I pushed that thought aside because I was too interested to do otherwise. I pulled out the letter that was lying on top. It was inside a crinkled envelope addressed simply to Maggie.

I remembered Will had called my mother by that name.

There was a number one in the upper right-hand corner, so it seemed like a good place to start. I opened up the aged letter with trembling hands and began to read.

Dear Maggie,

I know you probably don't know me, but my name is Max. We're in first period English class together. I know you're kind of shy, and you seem to like keeping to yourself, so I hope this doesn't scare you off. I think you're really pretty, and you also seem nice, and not at all like the other girls. I hope you don't take that the wrong way. I think it's a good thing that you're different. What I would really like to know is if you would like to meet up at the library and study together sometime? You're really smart and always have the right answers in English class. I was hoping you could help me. Let me know.

Sincerely,
Max

I read and reread the letter, trying to picture my mom as a teenage girl. She'd obviously been different, even back then, according to Max. My interest was definitely piqued at this point, so I grabbed the box and carried it down to my room, leaving my own things in the attic. Somehow, they didn't seem half as interesting as the discovery of Mom's letters.

I curled up on my bed and began to read the letters, which were numbered from one to seventy. I was so engrossed in reading them that I didn't even realize it was beginning to get dark. I glanced at the bedside clock and was startled to see that it was nearly seven o'clock. I'd been reading for hours, completely immersed in the world I'd stumbled upon. I looked at the number of the letter I was on and realized I'd read half of them already.

I was amazed at this sweet romance my mother had experienced. The letters evolved over the course of her senior year in high school, and from what I'd discovered, she and Max were quite in love. Their relationship was serious, and had become so very quickly. I was shocked at the similarities between Mom's relationship with Max and mine with Sam. I hadn't yet gotten to the end, but since I'd never heard of Max, my assumption was that it hadn't ended happily.

I placed the letters back into the box and slid it under my bed. I still felt a bit guilty for intruding on something as private as Mom's love letters, but I couldn't bring myself to stop. I had to know how it ended. My stomach growled, reminding me that I should make something for dinner. Reluctantly, I left the world of Max and Maggie and headed downstairs, my mind still fixated on the letters. I couldn't wait to learn more about my mom and her first love. Perhaps knowing her better would help me understand how she ultimately became the bitter woman who raised me.

Chapter Eleven

The next morning, I sat on the front porch swing wrapped in a fleece blanket in an attempt to keep the chilliness at bay. I hadn't slept well, consumed all night with thoughts of my mother and Max. In my dreams, somehow my mother's love affair had morphed into my own relationship with Sam, and the result was sad and twisted. I was more than ready to wake up when the first glowing light of the day crept into my dark bedroom.

I sipped my coffee and neatly folded letter number fifty-three, gently placing it inside its envelope. I couldn't stop until I had answers. I was like a woman possessed now. The letter I'd just finished spoke about the first time Max and Maggie made love, and I found myself wiping away tears while reading the sweet words Max wrote. Physical intimacy was not something he'd taken lightly, and while I only learned Max's perspective from the letters, I couldn't help but think it would have been just as special for my mother.

It made me think of my own first time with Sam. We'd been sixteen; although we had been together for two years, we both wanted to wait until we were more mature. The night it happened, we didn't even plan it. It was just the natural progression of things. Making love to Sam only served to further cement him in my heart. Even after everything that had happened, I had no regrets about our intimacy.

From Mom's letters, I also learned that her parents had no idea she was involved with Max, and there was a high level of secrecy surrounding their relationship. Mom's father seemed to be something of a tyrant, and they were both very afraid of getting caught. My stomach clenched nervously with thoughts of how it would all end. I was completely wrapped up in her story, fully invested in learning the outcome. I felt a surge of empathy for my mother, knowing all too well how deeply the knife of a lost first love could cut.

I glanced up from the letters to see Bridget in her front yard. It was Saturday and not yet eight o'clock in the morning, so I gathered that Bridget and June weren't late sleepers. June seemed pretty structured, and I imagined she ran a rather tight ship. The little girl looked in my direction, and I waved as I caught her eye. She returned the wave, although halfheartedly. Her small shoulders were slumped, and she had a frown on her face, quite a change from the happy little girl she usually was. I kept the blanket wrapped around my shoulders and walked over to the fence.

"Morning, Bridget. How are you?" She ambled in my

direction, her head still hanging.

"I'm okay, I guess." Bridget shrugged, and I could see that she was clearly not okay.

"What's wrong, sweetie? You don't seem like your usual happy self this morning. Come on, it's Saturday! Shouldn't you be inside watching cartoons and eating Lucky Charms or something?" At least that's what I had done when I was her age.

"Lucky Charms? Are you kidding? Grandma June wouldn't let those things within a mile of our house. She says there is too much sugar and fake coloring in them. I should know… I ask for them every time we go to the grocery store." She rolled her eyes in exasperation. I stifled a grin.

"Well, I guess it's been a long time since I was a little girl. I'm not up on current child-rearing techniques, I suppose. Anyhow, what's wrong? I know it's something." I tried to draw the little girl out of her shell.

"Nothing important. Grandma June has to go to the store and I don't want to go. It's supposed to be sunny today, and I want to go to the beach, but she says she has errands to run. Going to the store stinks." Bridget crossed her arms, driving her point home.

"Well now, that is a problem. I've always hated running errands myself. I was just about to go for a walk on the beach. Do you think Grandma June would let you go with me?" I surprised myself with my suggestion.

"With you? Really? That would be cool. I'll go ask her."

Without a second's hesitation, Bridget ran inside the house. I stayed at the fence, assuming June would come out to talk with me. I started wondering where the little girl's parents were.

"Morning, Hope," June called as she came out the front door and walked over to me. "I apologize if Bridget was pestering you. I've told her to give you space, but she's so taken with you."

"Don't worry about that at all. I love Bridget's company. As a matter of fact, I've just offered to have her hang out with me for a while and accompany me for a walk on the beach while you run errands. It'll give you some time to yourself, and she will have more fun this way. That is, if it's okay with you, of course." I smiled at June and awaited her answer.

"Are you sure? That would make her awfully happy…." She trailed off and looked at Bridget and then back at me. I detected a strange expression on her face; it was a mixture of happiness and sadness at the same time. I wondered what it meant.

"Please, Grandma June, please? I don't wanna go to the dumb old store. Can I stay with Hope?" Bridget clasped her hands together and pleaded.

"I don't see why not if it's all right with Hope. I should only be gone a couple of hours." She nodded as if she'd come to some kind of conclusion in her mind.

"Bridget, you run inside and get a jacket. It's a cold morning and you'll freeze by the water." The instructions fell out of my mouth instinctively, and I giggled thinking how maternal I sounded.

"Hope's right. Warm clothes, little one. Off you go!" Bridget ran inside and June thanked me profusely for making the little girl's morning. I told her it would be fun for me, too. I was looking forward to spending some time with the little girl. I was anxious to learn more about her life.

Twenty minutes later, June was on her way to run errands, and Bridget and I were ambling happily through the dune grass toward the beach. I felt the sea spray on my face, and the moisture made my hair damp. The clouds were rolling back and the sunlight was peeking through, glistening like diamonds on the waves. This was such a lovely spot, and I wondered for about the thousandth time since my return how I'd been able to stay away from the ocean for so long.

The water fed my soul, and while my heart was still shattered, I could feel myself slowly beginning to heal. Returning home had been one of the most difficult decisions I'd ever made, and coming face-to-face with so many demons from my past was still a daily struggle. In spite of all of this, I was coming to realize that it was the best thing I could have done for my emotional state. I was getting to know myself and my mom in a way I'd never bothered to before. It was a slow, painful journey, but something told me it might just be worth it in the end.

Bridget walked beside me in silence, taking in the sights and sounds with the obvious appreciation of a native. She didn't stare with wide-eyed excitement and fascination, but absorbed it all with a kind of peaceful appreciation and certainty that this was her place in the world. This little girl was definitely an old soul. Perhaps that was the connection I felt with her. My sad upbringing and anxiety had made my childhood tough, and I never really fit in with my peers. I had a feeling that Bridget was dealing with a sadness of her own, although I didn't know exactly what it was.

"So, tell me, Bridget, do you live all alone in the house with your Grandma?" I wanted to know more about her, but didn't want to be too nosy either.

"Nah, Grandma June doesn't live with us. She just takes care of me sometimes, you know, like some kids go to day care while their parents work?" We arrived at the shoreline and Bridget and I sat down in the sand. We didn't even bother laying down a blanket. I kicked off my shoes and buried my feet in the sand, and she did the same.

I was more than a little bit surprised to learn that June didn't live next door. She seemed to always be there. "What about your parents? What do they do?" I was even more curious now. I'd assumed that she lived with June full-time. I'd never seen another adult there.

"Daddy is a commercial fisherman. He owns his own boat, and he's gone a lot right now for work. He has to support us, you know." Bridget picked up a stick and began to draw hearts in the sand. I was amazed at her level of maturity.

"Of course he does. It's nice that your Grandma June takes such good care of you when your parents are at work. What about your mom? What does she do?"

"My mom... well... she...." Bridget didn't finish the sentence, and I got the feeling she didn't want to talk about her mom. I knew all about difficult mother-daughter relationships, so I didn't push for more information, and she didn't give it.

"What about you? Where did you live before you came to help your mom?" Bridget turned the tables on me, and it took me by surprise.

"Well, I lived in New York for a lot of years, but I grew up here, in my mother's house. It's been a long time since I've been back, but my mom's sick and she needed my help. I'm glad I came back, though. You know, sweetie, as hard as you try, you can't outrun your problems." Bridget looked at me and nodded, as if she completely understood.

"I'm sorry your mom's sick, Hope. I'll bet she's really glad you're home." The little girl looked at me intently as she reached over and grasped my hand in her small one.

I didn't know how to respond. I wondered how a child could possibly understand exactly what I needed, but somehow she did. I tried to blink away the tears, but they had already started falling. I didn't want her to see me crying, but when I glanced in her direction, I saw her wiping away tears of her own.

Later that night, I settled into my bed to read more letters.

I'd been to visit Mom after the beach trip with Bridget. I was happy to learn she'd be coming home tomorrow, so I spent the rest of the afternoon cleaning the house in preparation. I knew how particular Mom was about having a spotless house, and I didn't want her to feel like she needed to do anything but rest when she came home.

Dr. Riddles warned us both that she had to take it easy, and I could tell from the frustrated look on Mom's face that was going to be difficult for her. Dr. Riddles was hoping to begin the chemotherapy as soon as she was fully healed from the surgery, and in order to heal, she had to give her body ample time to rest.

I was exhausted. I'd cleaned like a madwoman all afternoon, and the house smelled fresh and was ready for inspection. There wasn't a thing out of place, and I was proud of myself for the hard work. I was sure Mom would find something wrong with it, since my cleaning never met her high standards.

As soon as the thought entered my mind, I scolded myself. She had changed, and she really was trying to be more kind these days. I reminded myself to give her the benefit of the doubt. We couldn't make progress if I continued bringing up past wrongs.

I read five more letters before turning off the bedside lamp and willing myself to fall asleep. I lay in the darkness thinking about Max and wondering what became of him. I was amazed at the beautiful relationship Mom and he had shared. Each and every letter revealed a deep and mature love on both sides. They were preparing for a future together, and Max was already planning how they could be married after they graduated.

It seemed to me that Max was the romantic dreamer and my mother was the practical one. I was anxious to find out what had happened between them and why they never ended up together. I was coming to realize that I was more like my mom, at least in one area, than I ever knew. Neither of us got the happily ever after that our younger selves wished for.

Chapter Twelve

The next afternoon, Mom and I made the trip home from Ocean Beach Hospital in silence. I knew she was worried about being home while still unable to resume her normal life. She was upset and worried that it might be a year or more before she could return to work. It was going to be difficult for her to adjust to being taken care of, especially by me.

Before we left the hospital, Dr. Riddles pulled me into his office and warned me that she might become frustrated, and I was going to bear the brunt of that frustration. I actually smiled, and I knew Dr. Riddles was baffled by my reaction, but he didn't know the kind of relationship we had. I was used to her bitterness and anger; her frustration was normal for me. The thing that was hard to get used to was the new kindness and understanding we were learning. Even so, I was mentally prepared for an uphill battle, because I knew it was coming.

Mom stared out the window at scenery she'd seen every day of her life, but the look on her face was one of surprise and admiration, as if she were seeing it all for the very first time. I wondered if she felt like she'd been given a second chance at life. I knew that was how I would feel in her position.

"You must be anxious to get home, in your own bed. Being in the hospital is exhausting, all those nurses coming in at all hours to check on things." I tried to breach the silence with small talk, hoping to make her more comfortable and letting her know we were in this together.

"Yes, it will be good to get home." Mom turned her face away from the window and I felt her looking at me. "I'm grateful that you're here, Hope. I don't think you have any idea how much I appreciate all that you've done… considering… everything."

"You don't have to thank me. We're family, and that's what families should do." I removed my trembling right hand from the steering wheel and patted her bony one.

This was all so new to me, and I never felt like I knew the right words to say. It was a strange phenomenon, getting to know my own mother at almost thirty years old, but knowing she was just as much out of her element as I was made it a bit easier.

I pulled the car into the driveway, turned off the ignition, and walked around to the passenger side to help Mom out. She was weak, and her pain medication made her a bit dizzy at times. She offered me her frail arm, and I marveled at how tiny she had become. This disease had certainly taken its toll on her body already, and she had a long way yet to go. I offered up a silent prayer that she would be able to withstand it.

I helped her inside and, seeing how worn-out she was

just from the ride home, led her straight into the bedroom. I helped her undress, which was uncomfortable for both of us, but necessary. I reminded myself that this would all get easier as time passed.

"I know you're tired, Mom. I want you to just rest. Don't worry about anything. I'm going to run to Maxwell's and get some supplies to make dinner. I know you said you're not hungry, but you'll need to eat something when you wake up." I adjusted the covers on her body and placed her cell phone beside her. "Call me if you need me, but most of all, just sleep. Your body needs it."

She smiled weakly, nodded, and obediently closed her eyes. I locked the front door and made my way to the grocery store. When I arrived, I didn't waste any time; I grabbed a shopping cart and walked briskly down the aisles gathering ingredients for chicken noodle soup, not wanting to be gone too long. I was placing a bunch of carrots into the cart when I saw Will headed my direction.

"Hi there." I smiled.

"I'm glad to see you, Hope. I heard your mom got to come home today. How is she?" He didn't waste any time getting right to the point.

"Wow, I always forget what a small town this is. News travels fast, very fast." I was amazed that he already knew Mom had been released. That seemed quick, even for Woodridge.

He shifted his weight from foot to foot, and I noticed that he seemed a bit out of sorts. Come to think of it, he'd been acting strangely when I ran into him at the hospital the other day, too. I hoped everything was all right with him. He was such a nice man.

"How are you doing, Will? Are you feeling okay?" I didn't want to pry, but he was always so kind to me, and I got the distinct feeling that something was wrong.

"I'm fine. Just been a bit preoccupied with the store lately. Don't you worry about me, sweetheart. You have enough on your plate." He patted my shoulder and smiled kindly.

"If you're sure… I do need to get going. I'm making chicken noodle soup for Mom." I gestured at the ingredients in my shopping cart. "I'll tell her you asked about her."

"Yeah, sure, that would be just fine." He smiled, but again, it didn't quite reach his brown eyes. I was concerned about him, but told myself I was probably overreacting.

I loaded my groceries into the car and headed home to begin cooking. I looked in on Mom before I began, and was glad to find her sound asleep. I chopped carrots, celery, garlic, and onions, and delighted in the delicious aroma that filled the kitchen. I wasn't much of a cook, but soup was a specialty of mine; soup was comfort food.

While my concoction was simmering to perfection, I grabbed my cell phone and sent the e-mail I had been dreading for the past couple of days. I needed to honestly respond to Reena, with whom I'd been strategically avoiding the truth. It was time to own up to the fact that I hadn't written anything in months and beg for mercy.

I told her that I was slowly becoming myself again, even though that wasn't exactly accurate. I was actually becoming a new version of myself, and I was still getting to know that woman. I did promise her I would begin working on the new book tomorrow, and I would have the first few chapters to her within the next month. It felt good to tell her the whole truth.

Making a deadline had always worked in the past, and I hoped it would be the motivation I needed this time as well. I was standing in front of the stove stirring the soup when I heard Mom enter the kitchen.

"What are you making? It smells delicious." She had never complimented my cooking before, so I was taken by surprise.

"Chicken noodle soup. I thought it might taste good to you. I know it always helps me when I'm not feeling well." I didn't turn around.

"That was a great idea. You've become such a fine woman. I take absolutely no credit for it, of course, just in case you wondered." Mom cleared her throat. "I messed up terribly as a mother, and I regret it every day." She spoke quietly and I wondered for a minute if I'd imagined it.

My back was still turned to her, but I stopped stirring and stood stock-still. I'd never expected such a blatantly honest statement from my mother, and I wasn't sure what to say or do.

I slowly turned toward her and gulped as I tried to form the perfect words in my brain. It didn't work. Instead, the only thing that came out was, "Don't say that. You did the best you could."

"I told myself that for years, but I will say it because it's true. And please don't try to make me feel better. It's about time I owned up to the mess I made, don't you think?" She smiled timidly, but her voice was full of determination.

"We both made mistakes…," I stammered, not wanting to

admit what she was saying was the truth. I wasn't ready to feel all the pain her statement brought to the surface.

"Of course we both made mistakes. But the first and biggest mistake was mine. I made the mistake of not letting you into my heart. I held you at arm's length your whole life. I refused to give you the love and affection a little girl needed. Mostly it was because I never learned how, but I know now that was just an excuse. No wonder you ran the first chance you had." Mom began to pace, but she continued talking, almost as if she had to get it out before she lost her nerve.

I did my best to really listen to her words as they poured from her heart. "I tried to blame you. I tried for years to convince myself I was angry with you for leaving me, but really, I'm angry at myself for pushing you away. Getting sick has taught me something, Hope. We have no guarantee of tomorrow. So I need to tell you today that I love you. I'm proud of you. I always have been." She took a shuddering breath as she finished.

Suddenly, I felt as if I were five years old again—that desperate little girl wanting her mom's approval more than anything. In a million years, I never imagined my mom would give it to me. Layer upon layer of hurt and pain were built up like a wall inside of me. I'd held on to so much anger, using it as a crutch for as long as I could remember. And here she was, asking me to forgive her.

A month ago, I would have dismissed the possibility of forgiving my mother without a second thought. I would have said there was too much pain, and forgiveness just wasn't possible. Right now, though, looking at my frail mother, I knew

I wanted to forgive her more than I'd ever wanted anything in my life. Not only did I want to forgive her, I needed to. We'd been given a second chance, and I was going to reach out and grab it with all I had in me. There were a lot of things in my past I couldn't change, but this wasn't one of them.

Tears streaming down my face, I ran to her and threw my arms around her, sobbing as I poured out twenty-eight years' worth of pain. My body shook as I held on to her. She held me tightly, cradling me in her thin arms and whispering soothing words. For the first time in my life, I felt connected to her. I had no idea that my mom's arms could be such a safe haven, and I cried for the little girl who had needed her so much. Mom and I stood in the kitchen as we had hundreds of times, but for the first time it felt like my home. For the first time, I didn't feel the need to run away.

I pulled away from Mom and wiped my eyes, and I saw that her face was just as streaked with tears as mine. She looked at me expectantly, and I knew exactly what I had to do. "I love you, Mom, and I forgive you."

As soon as I said those powerful words, I felt as if a huge chunk of my heart shifted back into place.

Chapter Thirteen

The next morning, bright sunbeams streamed through the lace curtains on my window, and upon opening my eyes I realized I was actually anticipating the new day. After hashing out a lifetime of painful memories with Mom last night, I'd gone upstairs and collapsed, drained. I slept like a rock. This morning I felt more rested than I had in months, obviously a result of making peace with a very uncomfortable part of my past.

It felt like a weight was lifted off my shoulders, and I honestly believed a miracle took place last night. I would have never believed that Mom and I could bridge the lifelong chasm between us; but somehow we were doing it.

I rolled out of bed, pulled on jeans and my old Seattle Mariners sweatshirt, flipped my hair into a messy bun, and headed straight for the coffeepot. I couldn't function properly without my morning java, and in spite of the wonderful thing that took place last night, I still needed caffeine.

When I glanced at the clock on the stove, I was surprised that Mom was still asleep. It was nearly eight thirty, and she never slept past seven. It was probably good for her. She needed as much rest as she could get. Deciding not to wake her, I grabbed my mug and headed out to the porch swing. It was a rare sunny day, not a common occurrence in Woodridge; I was going to soak up the vitamin D while it lasted.

I was desperate to read more Max and Maggie letters, but didn't want Mom to catch me with them. I'd left the box upstairs beneath my bed, and my fingers practically itched to hold them. I was so engrossed in their love story, and I couldn't wait to find out the end, but I knew I had to be patient. With her home it would be much more difficult to squeeze in private letter reading time. I would just have to do it at night before I went to sleep.

I sipped my coffee and thought about the things I needed to accomplish. I'd promised Reena that today was the day I would begin the new book, but I was still waiting for an idea to strike. Normally, I had no less than ten storylines bouncing around in my head, but lately, I couldn't seem to focus on anything other than my own troubles. My real-life issues were taking up too much space in my brain to leave any room for fiction. Nevertheless, it was my job, and I had a contractual obligation to produce. So I picked up the fresh notebook I'd purchased yesterday and my favorite pen and hoped for lightning to strike.

As I listened to the sound of the waves crashing in the distance, a thought began to swirl around in my head. *Write your story.* I tried to ignore it, but it wouldn't let up. *Write your story.* It was something I'd never before considered, and I nearly dismissed it altogether, but instead I decided to listen. In all my years as a writer, I'd never written anything that even remotely resembled my own life. I'd never wanted to. Lately, though, I had been so consumed with reality that focusing on fictional characters seemed impossible; I wondered if I could somehow combine fact and fiction.

Maybe the reason I wasn't bombarded by story ideas was because I was supposed to write my reality. The things that had happened to me over the last few weeks haunted me to the point where I couldn't think of anything else. I'd been frustrated by this fact, angry that it was interfering with my work. But what if I used it to help me come to terms with my life? Writing had always been therapy for me, mostly because it allowed me to escape my reality and make a new one. But what if I wrote this book to help me deal with my reality instead of trying to escape it? The thoughts circled around and around in my head like a hamster on a wheel.

Like a slow, rolling boil, a plot began to form. Characters and storylines paraded through my head, screaming at me to listen to them. I jotted ideas onto the paper in front of me, not dismissing anything that presented itself. This was vastly different from my normal writing method, but I was intrigued enough to go along for the ride.

With sudden clarity, I knew I was on the right path. Of course, I wouldn't exactly write my story; it wouldn't be autobiographical. I certainly wouldn't make it completely true, and a lot of things I would work through differently or leave out entirely. But I could use some of the problems I'd dealt with in the book. My characters and I could work through it all together. The idea began to solidify and my brain and my pen took off. This was a totally new approach for me, but I had a feeling it could very well become my best work to date. It would be relatable and relevant, two things that made a book great.

I began writing like a madwoman. The ideas flowed out of my head and through my hand in a steady stream. I felt as if I'd turned on a faucet. Glancing at the clock on my cell phone, I was astonished to find I'd been writing for over two hours. It felt like I'd only just begun.

I took a sip of my coffee, which was now ice cold, and closed my notebook with a feeling of satisfaction. This was going to be a story unlike any other I'd written, but somehow I knew it would work. I breathed a sigh of relief that I could finally let Reena know I was back on track.

I was just about to go inside to check on Mom when I saw June walking toward the fence between our yards. I smiled at her and gave a little wave.

"Morning, June."

"Good morning, dear. It looks like you've been hard at work." June nodded toward my notebook.

"Yes, I'm hot on the trail of my new book. It's one of the best feelings in the world." I beamed, hugging my notebook close to my chest. It was the truth, and I was happy to be doing what I loved once again.

"I can't imagine coming up with all of those stories in my head. It's an amazing talent you have, young lady." She shook her head in amazement.

"Thanks, but it's such a part of who I am, I never really view it as anything spectacular." I shrugged.

"Don't sell yourself short, my dear. It certainly is spectacular. How is your mother?"

"She's doing well, all things considered. I'm glad I'm here to help her."

"I'll bet she's glad, too." June paused, seeming to contemplate her next words.

"I hate to bother you with another thing, but I have a doctor's appointment this afternoon and I don't want Bridget to have to go with me. She hates waiting for me, and I can't say I blame her. She has the day off from school, and sitting at the doctor's office isn't how she wants to spend it." June's brow furrowed as she continued on. "Usually, I try to schedule my appointments around when her father is home, but this time it just didn't work out. He's been so busy lately with fishing season. I was wondering if you might be able to come over and sit with her. If it's too much trouble, just say so, dear."

"I don't see why that would be a problem at all. I'll make sure Mom is settled, and then head over around lunchtime, if that works. It's not like I'll be far away if she needs me, and I'd love to spend the afternoon with Bridget."

"That's wonderful news. Bridget will be ecstatic. You know, she likes you so much and she's not one who's usually comfortable around new people. There's just something about you that she trusts, I guess." June had the same strange look on her face that I'd seen the other day when I asked if

Bridget could come to the beach with me.

I got the distinct feeling that she was attempting to come to terms with something, but was having a difficult time. I sensed a definite internal struggle in the woman, but I had no idea why. Maybe she was just worried about leaving Bridget alone with me.

I wanted to ask her what was troubling her, but as quickly as I noticed the look, it was gone. She continued chatting. "And in exchange for watching Bridget, I'm happy to give you a break and come over and sit with your mom whenever you need to get away. All you have to do is ask."

"Thanks, June. I may take you up on that at some point. I'm going to go inside and check on her. I'll come over around noon so you can leave for your appointment." I waved good-bye to her and went in the house.

June exuded genuine kindness. It practically floated like a cloud above her head and made me wish I could follow her around and soak it in. I was really glad I'd met her and Bridget.

Happily, I found Mom sitting at the kitchen table sipping hot tea. There was an empty plate in front of her, so I assumed she'd eaten something, which was progress. Her appetite was lacking lately, and Dr. Riddles had warned us both that she needed proper nutrition in order to heal from the surgery. I suspected that worry was a factor in her lackluster desire for food. She was nervous about starting the chemo in a couple of weeks, and she wasn't the only one.

I'd heard horror stories of the terrible things people went through during chemotherapy. I hoped I had the patience and the strength to help her get through it. I knew the process would either make our fledgling relationship stronger, or destroy it altogether.

"Morning, Mom." I leaned down and kissed the top of her head. She smiled up at me. "Did you sleep well?" I carried my coffee mug to the sink, rinsed it, and loaded it into the dishwasher.

"I slept like a rock, better than I've slept in months." She gathered her dishes and carried them to the sink. I grabbed them from her, rinsed them, and then placed them into the dishwasher as well. "You looked like you were pretty engrossed in something out on the porch swing, so I didn't want to interrupt you when I woke up. Was it work?"

"It was. With everything that's happened in my life lately, I've had a hard time beginning the new book I should have started months ago. My agent told me in no uncertain terms that vacation time is over, and I'm happy to say that I made some progress this morning. I know exactly what I'm going to do with the story." I smiled and the excitement I'd felt earlier grew a little more.

"That's good, honey. I've read everything you've ever written. I'm not sure if I ever told you that or not. You're quite a gifted writer. It's no wonder you top all the best-seller lists." Mom patted me on the arm.

"I didn't know you'd ever read any of my books." I was startled at her revelation. I'd had no idea she'd kept up on my career or read my work.

"Well, I have. And I'm glad you're back to doing what you love. It's your gift, you know." Mom cleared her throat, obviously uncomfortable talking so intimately with me, but determined to do so anyhow.

She continued. "It's been a rough few months for you, hasn't it? I've been so focused on myself that I never even bothered to ask you how you're handling everything. Do you want to talk about it?"

"Um… well… I don't know…. It might help…." I went to the table and sat down; she followed. Never in my life had I talked to my mother about personal things, and my stomach fluttered at the thought of revealing my intimate thoughts. But at the same time, I was curious to know what a mother-daughter heart-to-heart conversation felt like. I supposed I was about to find out.

"What happened with you and Jonathan? You never said specifically, only that you were no longer together." Mom reached across the table and grabbed my hand. It was just the impetus I needed to begin.

"A couple of months ago, I found out I was pregnant. Jonathan and I were so happy. I actually thought I couldn't have children because I'd never conceived, even though we hadn't done anything to prevent it. So it was a surprise, but a good one. I thought things were fine, but then I found a note in his pocket from one of his students. He'd been having an affair for months, apparently, and I was completely oblivious." I stopped and took a deep breath. My heart raced as I relived the event, trying not to cry. I wasn't sure how many details to divulge.

"Oh, honey…." Mom squeezed my hand and I continued.

"So I kicked him out. I knew I could never trust him again. Don't get me wrong, our marriage wasn't perfect, but I thought I could trust him. When I found out he was cheating, it was the end for me. A couple of days later, I started cramping. It hurt so badly. Then I started to bleed… and I… I knew…. I lost… I knew I lost the baby." I couldn't hold back the tears anymore, and they began to fall.

She gathered me into her arms and let me cry. It was excruciating to think of my baby, and the grief that filled me up inside began to pour out. I'd held it in for so long, and it felt good to unburden myself. Having Mom's comforting arms around me was exactly what I needed. I felt safe, protected, and not alone.

"Sweetie, I'm so sorry that happened to you. I've never lost a baby, so I can't say that I understand, but I do know what grief feels like. I wish I had some words of wisdom to give you, but I don't. All I can say is I'm here, if you need someone to listen. Or hold you when you need it." Mom wiped the tears from my face with her trembling hands.

"Thanks. It feels good to talk about it. I can't believe I'm saying that, but it's true. Holding it in hurts so much. It feels toxic. I think about the baby every single day. I'd probably be showing by now if I was still pregnant… maybe feeling the baby move… I've lost so much." I couldn't bring myself to say any more, so I stopped. "I guess some things just weren't meant to be."

"You're so young, Hope. You're not even thirty years old yet. You have no idea what the future has in store for you. Don't give up on your happy ending." Mom hugged me again.

"I don't know. Jonathan and I would never have lasted

even if none of the rest happened. I never loved him how he needed to be loved, and we both knew it from the beginning. If I'm honest, it was all just as much my fault as it was his. I never gave him my heart. I couldn't—" I didn't continue.

Mom looked confused at my abrupt stop, but didn't push me. Instead, she stood up from the table to finish loading the dishwasher, allowing me to regain control.

I'd just revealed a lot to Mom, but I wasn't ready to tell her about Sam. She didn't know that we were once involved. She knew him. He had been our neighbor for years, but I never told her we were in love. I was emotionally depleted from talking about my miscarriage and impending divorce, and I didn't have enough energy to begin that story, so I changed the subject completely.

"Do you think you'll be all right alone here this afternoon, Mom?"

"I think so. Is there something you need to do? I know that taking care of me has consumed your time lately. I'm sorry about that."

"Don't be ridiculous. Believe it or not, there's no place else I'd rather be." I chuckled to myself as I said the words I never thought I'd say. "It's just that June, from next door, has a doctor's appointment and I said I'd go over and sit with Bridget so she could go. There's no school today, so they had a bit of a conflict. I'll just be next door if you need anything."

Mom's forehead crinkled a bit and her mouth turned upside down into a slight frown. It was a strange reaction. She seemed to measure her words before she spoke. "I wasn't aware that you knew Bridget and June."

"We've been talking a bit here and there. June is a sweetheart, and Bridget is a fantastic little girl. I really like spending time with her. She reminds me of someone, but I can't quite put my finger on it."

"Yes, they're both very nice." Mom looked concerned, but all she said was, "Just be careful, Hope."

"Be careful? With what, Mom? Babysitting Bridget? I think I can handle it." I laughed at her strange behavior.

"Not with babysitting. Just… I worry about you… that's all." Mom turned her back to me. I could tell she wanted to say something more, but she didn't. I decided not to push the issue because when I glanced at the clock I saw it was time to go.

"I'll be less than a hundred feet away. What could possibly go wrong? Call me if you need anything at all." I grabbed my phone and walked next door, ignoring the worried expression on my mother's face as I left. She must have been out of sorts because of her illness. That would explain her odd behavior and peculiar warnings.

When I arrived, June called me around to the backyard. I entered the house through the back door, which led directly into the kitchen. June hugged me and thanked me profusely for helping her out of a jam. After she left, I closed the door and asked Bridget how she wanted to spend the afternoon.

"Can you bake?" Bridget asked quietly.

"Well, I'm not Betty Crocker, but I do all right. What do you have in mind?"

"Grandma June does so much for me. I thought maybe it

would be nice to bake her some cookies. Can we do that?"

"I think that's a great idea, Bridget. Let's be sure you have all the ingredients." She was so sweet and thoughtful. I grabbed her hand and she led me to the pantry.

The kitchen was immaculate, but that was really no surprise considering the amount of time June spent there. I had to admit it was a bit jarring to be back inside this room I remembered so well. I'd spent a large chunk of my teenage years here with Sam, and very little had changed. When Bridget's family bought the house, they certainly hadn't done many renovations in this room. The kitchen had the exact same wallpaper as it had ten years ago. The crystal chandelier I'd always admired still hung on the ceiling above the large antique table, which I could have sworn was the same one Sam's parents had.

I tried to ignore the pain as I thought about all the time I'd spent here with Sam, hanging out in his room, studying, and having dinner with his parents. I tried to push the memories aside; I didn't want to upset Bridget. She was so excited to spend the afternoon with me, so I plastered a smile on my face and helped her look for cookie ingredients.

We spread everything out on the counter and started mixing the dough. I told Bridget she could do it all and I would be her assistant. She giggled and I could tell she was excited about the idea. I soon discovered that she was quite a good little baker, and I guessed that June had given her a lesson or two. She placed the dollops of cookie dough on the tray, and I popped it in the oven for her. She began placing dough on another tray, but we both stopped when we heard a vehicle pull into the driveway.

Glancing at the clock, I saw that it was just over an hour since June left. "It sounds like your grandma's home already. I didn't expect her back so soon."

The front door opened and closed, and I called out, "We're in the kitchen, June." I helped Bridget begin the second tray of cookies while we waited for June to find us.

I reached down and closed the bag of flour, and as I did, a white cloud of it escaped the bag and collected on my nose. I sneezed and Bridget and I burst out laughing. She grabbed a towel and attempted to help me wipe my face.

We were both giggling as we heard footsteps enter the kitchen. I glanced up, a smile on my face, expecting to see June. What I saw instead stopped me dead in my tracks. I grabbed the counter as my knees practically buckled beneath me, the shock nearly too much to digest.

"Daddy! You're home! I didn't think you'd be back until tomorrow!" Bridget dropped the spoon of cookie dough and ran, catapulting herself into the arms of the large man who'd entered the room.

The blood drained from my head, and for a moment, everything went black. I told myself not to pass out, and it was nothing short of willpower that kept me on my feet. I blinked my blurry eyes twice, certain I must be hallucinating.

"Sam?" His name escaped my lips before I could pull it back, and my hands flew to my mouth to stifle the sound, but it was too late.

I was trapped, staring in disbelief not at an apparition but the flesh-and-blood man I'd thought I'd never see again.

There was no escape, nothing at all I could do. I looked helplessly into the eyes of my first love, somehow beginning to understand that Sam was Bridget's father.

I looked at the two of them standing side by side, and in that instant, I realized why I'd felt so connected to Bridget. With her white-blonde hair and baby-blue eyes, she was the spitting image of Sam. They had the same mannerisms, the same knowing expression, and they even stood the same way, staring at me with identical confused looks on their faces. Somehow I must have known, somewhere deep inside of me, that she was his daughter.

"Hope? Is that you?" Sam finally spoke, and when he did, I was transported back in time. His voice was achingly familiar, even after all these years. And it hurt immensely to hear him say my name.

"Daddy, do you know Hope?" Bridget, obviously confused by the tension that filled the room, looked back and forth between Sam and me.

"Yes, we know each other very well." Sam spoke to Bridget, but never took his penetrating eyes off me.

It was too much. My brain churned furiously, trying to take it all in. There wasn't enough oxygen in the room, and I was fighting for air. I had to get out of there. Bridget looked at me with a worried expression, and the only thing that kept me from collapsing into a puddle on the kitchen floor was her sweet little face.

"Bridget, I'm not feeling well. I need to go now that your… daddy… is home." It was all I could do to get the words out before I ran from the kitchen.

"Hope! Come back!" Sam called to me as I sprinted out the front door, but I didn't turn around. Instead, I ran as if the devil himself were chasing me.

The tears began to fall, like large splattering raindrops down my cheeks. I fumbled with the doorknob and burst into my house, running right past Mom and her startled expression. I didn't stop; I couldn't. I kept running until I was upstairs in my room, where I slammed the door behind me and collapsed on my bed, my body shaking violently as bottled-up grief and pain came pouring out.

Chapter Fourteen

Two hours later, the sobs were still coming; I took ragged breaths and tried to dam the flood of tears that seemed to have no end. Pulling myself off the bed, I walked across the room to the vanity table, where I grabbed a handful of tissues and plopped down on the faded flowered cushion. Glancing at myself in the mirror, I was aghast at the train wreck staring back at me.

My blonde hair, which I'd casually swept up in a messy bun that morning, was now sprawling haphazardly in every direction. Some of the strands escaped and were plastered to my tear-soaked cheeks. I pushed them back, mortified at my pathetic appearance. My eyes were swollen and puffy from crying, and I looked like I'd been punched in the face. I swallowed over the lump in my throat that seemed to have taken up permanent residence.

Nothing could have ever prepared me for finding out that Bridget was Sam's daughter. Never in a million years did I think I would see Sam again, let alone babysit his child. I hadn't laid eyes on the man in over ten years, but seeing him again made me feel as if no time had passed.

I finally understood why I'd been drawn to Bridget from the first time I saw her. She was identical to Sam in nearly every way, and I was shocked I hadn't picked up on it sooner. Or maybe I had on some level, and I had just refused to admit it to myself. *Sam, my true love.* The words played over and over in my mind, the image of him walking into the kitchen stuck on repeat in my brain. I couldn't believe I'd seen him again. It was like a bad dream.

I had to admit that time had been more than kind to Sam. He'd been a good-looking boy, but he'd grown into an exquisitely handsome man. He wore his white-blond hair a little longer than when he was young, but the wildness of it suited him. His thin, wiry teenage body had been replaced by the physique of a hardworking man. His shoulders were wider, his arms were muscular, and the only trace of the boy I used to know was in his baby-blue eyes that still sparkled like the ocean on a sunny day. The same eyes that had widened in surprise when he saw me standing in his kitchen with his daughter; the very same eyes in which I used to get lost, where once upon a time I saw my future.

How was it possible that I hadn't known Sam lived in his parents' old house? Kelsey had lost touch with things around Woodridge once her parents moved, but it seemed crazy that no one mentioned Sam and his family lived next door to my mother. *His family.* Those words caused my mind to race in a thousand different directions. The last I heard,

Sam and Annie had planned to be married after graduation, and I'd always just assumed they'd lived happily ever after with their baby. Sam had always been adamant that he never intended to stay in Woodridge, and once I heard his parents' house was for sale, I made the assumption that he had left town.

Bridget was Sam and Annie's daughter, the baby conceived because of their one-night stand. Bridget, the little girl I'd come to adore, was the daughter of the woman who I'd once blamed for ruining my life. Although my feelings toward Annie had mellowed a bit over the years, she was still a sore spot in my mind. It was a lot to wrap my head around.

It seemed like the hits just kept on coming in my world. Every day there was some new battle for me to fight, and I didn't know how much more I could take. Fresh tears began to fall and my body shook with sobs. Without another thought, I grabbed my phone and dialed Kelsey's number. She picked up on the third ring, but I was crying so hard I couldn't speak.

"Hope… honey… is that you? Are you there?" Kelsey's concerned voice was like a giant hug reaching right through the phone line.

"I… saw… him…." I tried to get the words out, but I was practically hyperventilating. I knew I was making no sense.

"Saw who? Hope, take five deep breaths with me, come on…." My patient best friend breathed in and out on the other end of the line, and I followed. After the fifth breath I'd finally gained a little composure.

"Sam. I saw Sam." At the mention of his name, my voice quivered and it took all the effort I had to hold it together. "He lives next door. I met his daughter, but I didn't know she was his daughter…. I like spending time with her…. What am I going to do?"

Through ragged breaths, I managed to explain the situation to Kelsey, who listened sympathetically while I broke down once again. After talking me off the ledge for the third time, she dove right into Mama Bear mode and gave me the "tough love" pep talk I so obviously needed.

"You, my dear, are going to suck it up and pull yourself together. You are a strong woman, Hope West. You're stronger than you've ever given yourself credit for. You will not allow yourself to fall apart. Your mom needs you, and look at all the progress you've made since you went home. Are you going to let the fact that Sam lives next door destroy all of that? I'll answer for you… no, you're not."

"I know, Kel. It's just… I never expected to see him again. It's hard enough that he's in control of my brain, and now he lives next door? With his wife and daughter? It's a little much, don't you think?" I blew out an exasperated breath.

"Well, you could just avoid him. Right?" She had a logical answer for everything. My feelings were anything but logical.

"I could, but what about Bridget? We've gotten really close. That wouldn't be fair to her. She's just a kid. None of this is her fault."

"What about Annie? What's she like after all this time? She always was a wild child. I can't imagine her as a mother."

My loyal best friend had never liked Annie. She wasn't the only one.

"Honestly, I have no idea. It's the strangest thing. Bridget never talks about her, and I haven't ever seen her. She must work a lot. I was only in the kitchen today at Sam's house, so I didn't get the chance to look around. I didn't see any photos or anything. I hope she got old and ugly." I laughed at my own mean thoughts, realizing that I sounded like a bratty kid when I said it.

"Well, she never was as pretty as you, anyhow. Sam certainly messed up when he lost you."

"Thanks, Kel, but we both messed up, me more than him. When are you coming to see me? I really need you now."

"Soon. Within the next couple of weeks. I'm arranging my schedule as we speak. In the meantime, just take it one day at a time, sweetie. Call if you need me."

"Okay, love you." I hung up the phone and took a deep breath. I needed to explain things to Mom, who must have been wondering what was wrong with me.

I went downstairs and found her sitting on the living room couch quietly flipping through a magazine. She glanced up and patted the seat beside her; I obediently sat down. She put her arm around me, and I laid my exhausted head on her shoulder while I told her the whole story, this time not leaving anything out.

If Mom was surprised by my revelation about Sam being my first love, she didn't let on. I was beginning to understand that there was more to my mom than I'd ever imagined. I had a feeling she'd known all along that Sam and I were in love.

"That's why you warned me to be careful today, isn't it?" Realization dawned on me.

"Yes. I had no idea that you were friends with Bridget and June, and I wasn't sure whether or not you knew Sam was Bridget's father. I didn't want to be the one to tell you, but now I wish I had. At least you wouldn't have been caught off guard this afternoon." Mom's face was full of sadness.

"How long has Sam been back? I thought he must have moved away after his parents died."

"He did. The house was on the market for about a year after his parents died in the car accident, but it never sold. Sam was living in Seattle, working on a fishing boat, but decided to move back to town and live in the house himself, I guess. Bridget was just a tiny little thing when they moved in. I don't really talk to him much, but he is a nice young man. He helps me with yard work and things around the house every once in a while. I'm sorry I never mentioned it to you."

"This is a lot for me to take in. I don't think you understand how much he meant to me, Mom. I'll never love anyone the way I loved him. That was the root of all the problems I had with Jonathan. He always knew he couldn't compete with Sam, even though he had no idea who he was."

"I might understand more than you think, Hope. I've always heard that you never really get over your first love, and I believe that might be true."

This seemed like the perfect opportunity to ask about Max, but I was so wrapped up in my own pain that I didn't. I wanted to know all I could about Sam and Annie, but I wasn't sure if Mom had all the answers.

"So… June… is Annie's mom?" As I said the words, a sinking feeling settled in my stomach.

"Yes, she is. But there's something else you should know about Annie—" Mom started.

I cut her off. "No more tonight, Mom. I think I've experienced all that I can process right now." I was having a hard time handling the fact that June, the kind woman I adored, was the mother of the girl I once blamed for taking Sam away from me. It was hard to believe that the wild, reckless Annie I remembered could be June's daughter or Bridget's mother. Maybe motherhood had changed her. June obviously had no idea about my past with Sam. I couldn't imagine she would want Sam's old girlfriend around her granddaughter. Annie had never liked me, so I wouldn't be her first choice of a companion for her child either.

There were so many unanswered questions, but my mind and body were too exhausted to ponder them all at that moment. Even though it was still early, all I wanted to do was sleep away the pain.

"I'm beat, Mom. I'm going to shower and go to bed now. I'll see you in the morning." I kissed her good night, took a quick shower, and crawled into bed. Before turning out the bedside lamp, I glanced out the window toward Sam's house next door. I saw a shadow move behind the curtains of the upstairs bedroom and I wondered if he was thinking of me like I was thinking of him.

Chapter Fifteen

The next afternoon, Mom was in her bedroom napping and I was at the kitchen table working on my book. I yawned, feeling like I'd been awake for days on end. I'd slept fitfully the night before and awakened early, unable to keep thoughts of Sam out of my head long enough to rest. So I started writing, hopeful that my characters would distract me. So far, I'd managed to write five more chapters, but I still couldn't stop thinking about Sam and Bridget.

I knew the entire situation was basically impossible. There was no easy answer. I was too attached to Bridget to simply pretend she didn't exist, but once Annie learned of our friendship, I was sure she would forbid Bridget to speak to me. Even if she didn't, I had no idea how I could be around Bridget, knowing Sam was her father. If I did run into him again, I wouldn't be able to conceal my feelings. My love for him would be written all over my face, obvious for the entire world to see.

I sighed, stopped typing, and rubbed my swollen eyes. They were still stinging from the hours of crying I'd done last night. I decided I needed more coffee, and was just about to brew a fresh pot when I heard someone knocking. I should have looked before I answered, but I didn't. I opened the front door, receiving a fresh punch in the gut when I saw Sam standing on the other side.

He smiled, but it was a smile filled with sadness. I'd always been able to read his thoughts, and I was astonished to find that I still could. I felt the despair inside him, so palpable that I could almost reach out and grab it. His emotions perfectly mirrored my own.

"Hope." Sam said my name, and it was as intimate as if he'd touched me. I wanted nothing more than to throw myself into his arms and tell him I loved him, but that was impossible.

"Sam, what can I do for you?" My voice sounded dead to my ears, and I marveled at how well I'd been able to conceal my feelings.

"I know you were just as surprised to see me as I was to see you yesterday. I had no idea you were back in town." Sam shifted nervously, chewing his lip the way he'd done when we were young. My arms ached to reach out and hold him.

"Yes, I've been back for a while now. I'm here to take care of my mother. She's ill." My voice was a monotone, conveying nothing of the turmoil inside me.

"I know. I'm sure she's glad to have you here." He cleared his throat, and his voice wavered. "There's so much to say…. I don't even know where to start…."

"Bridget is a lovely little girl. You and Annie must be so proud." I interrupted him before he could continue down the path that would lead to nothing but more heartbreak for me.

"Yes… we… I… am proud of her. She's pretty incredible. She's my whole world, really." Sam's face brightened at the mention of Bridget, and I knew he cared for her tremendously. I was glad. She deserved to have parents who loved her. Nothing about this messed up situation was her fault.

"Well, it looks like you have everything you ever wanted. I'm really happy for your family, Sam." I felt myself die a little bit more inside as I said the words out loud.

"I came over to see if we could talk, Hope. There are things you need to know." Sam's eyes met mine and I felt my resolve begin to crumble. I knew it was time to end this conversation before I said something that would embarrass us both.

"No, Sam, I don't think we need to talk. It seems to me that life has worked out just fine for you, so let's leave the past where it belongs. We've both moved on." My eyes filled with tears, and I knew I couldn't hold them back much longer.

"There are things I need to say, Hope. Things I should have said years ago. You don't need to say anything. Just listen."

"Sam… I can't… hear those things. You don't understand…." To my dismay, large tears began to fall one by one down my face.

He reached out and tentatively wiped them away, and I

shuddered at his touch. Like a magnet, my body was drawn to his and the next thing I knew, I was wrapped tightly in his arms. He was everything familiar to me, and for a moment, I pretended things were different. I closed my eyes and breathed in his scent, picturing the two of us happily in the future we'd wanted.

I tipped my face up and his fingers caressed my cheek. What was I doing? I knew I had to put a stop to this before I completely forgot the fact that he was no longer mine. "I need you to go home, Sam. Go home where you belong."

His face crumpled at my words, and for a moment, I feared the unshed tears in his eyes would break free. I could not watch his tears fall, so with one last glance, I stepped away from him and shut the door, breaking the connection between us. I saw his shadow through the curtains. He didn't leave; instead, his shoulders slumped and began to shake, and I knew he was crying.

I turned my back to the door and leaned against it, my legs giving out as I slid to the floor. When I looked at Sam, I wanted nothing more than to turn back the clock to that night long ago when I made the biggest mistake of my life. If I could do it all again, I'd never let him go. But I couldn't change things, and I wondered if I would ever get past it.

After a few minutes, his heavy footsteps retreated, and I stood up, wiping my face on my sleeve. I was so restless; I wanted to go outside for some fresh air. However, the chance of running into Sam, Bridget, or worst of all, Annie, made me realize that was a bad idea. I was trapped inside the house.

Mom was asleep, so on impulse I went up to the attic,

grabbed the box with my personal items inside, and carried it to my room. Opening the lid, I reached inside and took out a handful of photographs. I smiled as I saw images of Kelsey and me hamming it up for the camera.

I reached back into the box and pulled out one of my leather-bound yearbooks. Glancing at the date on the cover, I saw that it was from my freshman year of high school; the year I officially fell in love with Sam. I flipped through the pages and was transported back in time.

I traced my fingertip over a photo of us sitting next to each other in the school cafeteria. We hadn't known our picture was being taken, so neither of us was facing the camera. We were holding hands, and only had eyes for each other. Seeing how much in love we had been was like a knife in my chest.

I'd known Sam all my life; after all, we were neighbors. We said hello to each other and made small talk if we passed in the hallway, but he was always just another guy. The summer between eighth and ninth grade, though, something happened. He went away for the summer, and when he returned, I saw him in a whole new way. He seemed older, more mature, and I couldn't believe I'd never noticed how cute he was before.

I confided in Kelsey that I was interested in Sam, and she swore to keep my secret. I admired him from afar the first few weeks of school, doodling his name on my notebooks and trying to catch his eye as we passed each other between classes. I was shy, and Sam was popular; it seemed to me we were a pretty unlikely match, and I doubted if he even knew

I was alive. I would sit on my front porch, hoping he'd say something to me when he was outside. He smiled, but that was it. We never spoke.

At the first dance of the school year, my one and only goal was to get Samuel Mooney to notice me. I spent extra time on my hair and makeup. Mom wasn't willing to shell out any money for a new dress, so Kelsey, who was about four inches shorter than me, told me I could borrow one of hers. I stood in the corner of the high school gym, tugging on the purple dress that covered much less of my long legs than it did her petite ones. I knew it looked good on me, but I wasn't used to exposing so much skin. I'd dressed at the Norwoods', thankfully, knowing Mom would never let me out of the house in it. Kelsey assured me that I looked great, and I was just hoping Sam would look at me.

I stood beside her and watched Sam across the room as he laughed and joked with his friends. I silently begged him to notice me, and amazingly, it seemed to work. He looked my direction and made his way across the floor to where I stood. My heart thudded in my chest and my palms dripped with sweat; I couldn't believe my luck. I'd wished for him to ask me to dance, and there he was!

This was the moment I'd been waiting for. I smiled widely at him, ready to answer "Yes!" when he asked me to dance; the word was just sitting there on the tip of my tongue. To my utter dismay, Sam asked my best friend to dance instead. The color drained from her face as she looked helplessly at me, knowing how much I liked him. I loved her more than anyone else in the world, and I could never be mad at her, no matter how much it hurt that Sam asked her instead of me. So, I swallowed my pride and smiled encouragingly at her, even though I really wanted to run away crying.

As they walked to the dance floor, I held back tears of frustration and embarrassment. Of course Sam would ask her to dance. She was a fun, bubbly ball of energy. Everyone loved her. In contrast, I was awkward and shy; most people didn't even know I existed. I watched Sam and Kelsey sway to the music as they talked animatedly, glancing occasionally in my direction. I pretended to pick lint off my dress, needing something to do with my hands while I tried extra hard not to look as pathetic as I felt.

When the song ended, Sam glanced my way, said something to her, and returned to his friends. She strode swiftly toward me with a mile-wide grin on her face. I also plastered on a smile, not wanting her to know how hurt I was.

"Before you pretend you're happy for me, just listen." Kelsey, who knew me all too well, didn't let me get a word out.

"Listen to what?" I had no idea what she was talking about.

"He likes you." The smile on Kelsey's face was so big I thought it would swallow her whole.

"Who likes me? What are you talking about?"

"Sam, you dope. He likes you, not me. He was too shy to ask you to dance without knowing if you'd say yes or no. So he pumped me for information about you." Kelsey giggled and I thought for sure I was hearing things.

"Samuel Mooney likes me? He asked you about me? What did you tell him?" My heart beat wildly in my chest, and I felt like I'd just won the lottery.

"I told him if he asked you to dance you'd say yes. So he said on the next slow song he would." Kelsey talked a mile a minute and my brain struggled to keep up. "So don't chicken out when he comes over."

I nodded numbly as I heard the fast song end and a slow one begin. Sure enough, he walked toward me, a nervous smile on his handsome face. I gulped, telling the butterflies in my stomach to be still, and smiled back at him.

"Hope, will you dance with me?" Sam's voice, which was usually strong and steady, shook with nervousness.

"I'd love to, Sam." I was glad I sounded more confident than I actually felt.

He took my hand and led me to an empty spot on the dance floor. I felt lightheaded as he put his arms around my waist. Instinctively, I placed mine around his neck. We began to sway back and forth and I was certain my knees would give out. Luckily, they didn't.

"I'm glad you said yes. I've wanted to talk to you for a really long time, but I didn't figure a girl as pretty and smart as you would give me a second look." His eyes locked onto mine, and my nervousness vanished.

"I'm glad you asked, because I've wanted to talk to you for a really long time, too." I couldn't tear my gaze away from his if my life depended on it.

Sam and I danced to every song that night. It was the beginning of an intense friendship that quickly turned into a once-in-a-lifetime love. We were inseparable after that. Over the next three years, our love grew into something that I'd been hoping to find again ever since. I knew that Sam was it for me, which was why all these years later, I'd never figured out how to get over him.

Chapter Sixteen

A week later, Mom had recovered enough from her surgery to begin her first chemotherapy treatment. Dr. Riddles warned me privately that the procedure was going to be extremely hard on her, and that she would need my help now more than ever. The treatments would happen twice a week for the next three months.

She would become ill, tired, weak, and would most likely lose her hair. She would be highly susceptible to every germ around. Her brain would become foggy, and it would be difficult for her to remember simple things. It was my job to convince her that it would all be worth it once she was cancer free. I knew that supporting her through it would be one of the most difficult things I'd ever done.

On top of that, I was still reeling from my own personal crises. I'd managed to avoid Sam, Bridget, Annie, and June so far, but I knew my lucky streak wouldn't last forever. Eventually, I would have to deal with the situation; I wasn't looking forward to that day. To make matters worse, Jonathan was also giving me grief, calling nearly every day, begging me to talk to him. I screened his calls, sending him directly to voice mail, but he was making an already heartbreaking situation even more so.

He'd sent obnoxiously large flower arrangements on two separate occasions, and the smell of them nauseated me. I responded to him via e-mail both times, politely thanking him and telling him to stop. Yesterday, I received a delivery of an outrageously expensive painting that I'd had my eye on for years. I shipped it directly back to him.

He really was pulling out all the stops. He just wouldn't give up. Now he was refusing to sign the divorce papers, certain he could somehow convince me to change my mind. I didn't understand why he couldn't just resign himself to the fact we were over; that we had never been right for each other in the first place. More than anything, I just wanted him to go away, so I could move past that painful part of my life.

The only bright spot in my life was the Max and Maggie letters. I'd read all of them except the last three, which I'd smuggled into my bag this morning. Mom would be hooked up to her treatment for the next couple of hours, so I brought them along to keep me entertained in the waiting room.

As I unfolded the next letter, I realized it was different from the rest. It wasn't from Max, but from Mom, and it looked like it was never sent. My stomach tightened with anticipation as I began to read.

My Darling Max,

I have news, life changing news. After you read this, our world will never be the same again. You see, once the words are spoken, they can never be taken back. Once you know, you can never un-know, and that knowledge will force you to make choices I don't want you to have to make. I'm pregnant. Our lives will never again be carefree and filled with promise. We will be parents. Another human being will depend on us for its very existence. How can I ask you to give up your future? You have such a promising life ahead of you—a football scholarship! It would be so selfish of me to expect you to give that up for a family you never planned. So I won't. I won't ask that of you. I want you to be free to pursue your dreams, unburdened by me and a child. I love you more than life itself, Max, and I won't be the reason you're chained to this town. Good-bye, my love.

Yours Forever,
Maggie

I read and reread the letter several times as the words began to sink in. My mother had been pregnant. With me. The letter was still in the box with all the rest, so that meant she never sent it. Max never had the chance to read her words. My hands trembled as I pulled out the next letter. I hoped it would answer all the questions swirling around in my brain.

Maggie,

I don't understand what's happening. You won't return my calls. You won't answer my letters. I even came to your house to see you and you wouldn't answer the door. I know you were home; I saw you through the window as I left. What did I do wrong, Maggie? You know I love you. I love you more than my own life. You're my whole world. What about our plans? We'll be graduating soon and then your parents can't stop us from getting married. It's what we've always talked about, and it's so close. Don't you love me, Maggie? Please tell me what I did wrong so I can x it. I will love you forever.

Max

I released the breath that I'd been holding as I read the letter. The pieces of the puzzle were beginning to become clear in my mind, but I continued on to the very last letter, hoping for a happy ending even though I knew it wasn't to be.

Maggie,

Your silence speaks volumes. I don't know what I've done wrong, so I can't x it. I don't want to be a burden to you if your feelings for me have changed, so I will leave you alone. you obviously don't love me anymore. Just know that I'll always love you. That is one thing you cannot control.

Max

I couldn't believe it. Mom never told Max the truth. She was pregnant with me, and rather than tell him, she broke things off without explanation. Max, the mysterious man who was my mother's first love, was also my father. I let that thought percolate in my brain for a few moments.

I was beginning to have my suspicions about the mysterious Max. I'd always believed my father was a deadbeat who skipped town and abandoned Mom when he found out she was pregnant with me. Now I had to grapple with the possibility that maybe he never knew about me. My mother hadn't sent the letter explaining the pregnancy. Instead, she'd broken up with him without a single word as to why. Max might have had no idea he was my father. I wondered, if he'd known, how different my life might have been.

The revelation brought about conflicting feelings in me. My first impulse was anger toward Mom for robbing me of my father and Max of his daughter. I let the anger bubble inside for a while; I felt it, and I didn't push it away. Along with that anger came hurt. I couldn't believe all the years I'd felt unwanted. Watching my friends with their fathers was like a knife in the heart. How I'd ached to know what it felt like to have one! My mother stole that away from me.

Then another thought began to emerge. I put myself in Mom's shoes, and when I did, I understood that she'd made her decision out of genuine love for Max. She didn't want to be the anchor that tied him to Woodridge. He had a football scholarship, a chance to make something of himself. She must have known he'd have given it all up for her, but she didn't want him to. When I looked at it that way, it wasn't selfish; it was selfless.

My mother did the hard part of raising me alone. She had no help; her parents packed up and moved to Hawaii, leaving their home and my mother behind. I wondered now if it was due to having a daughter who was pregnant out of wedlock. I knew that I wasn't born until after Mom graduated from high school, but certainly people in town could tell she was pregnant. There must have been speculation about who my father was. Is that when she started to withdraw from society? From the bits and pieces I'd garnered about my grandparents, they were terribly strict and hard to please. Mom said they signed the house over to her and she never heard from them again. It was hard for me to imagine that they could completely abandon their daughter when she was pregnant, but at least they left her with a house, not out on the streets.

Mom had somehow put herself through nursing school while raising me. She never dated, and she had no social life. All she did was go to work and come home. No wonder she was bitter. It all made sense to me now.

I sat in the waiting room, wrestling with the emotions that the letters brought to the surface. Mom had never talked about my father, and I had never asked. I'd made a lot of assumptions about the kind of man he was based upon his absence, but I realized now that those conclusions may have been wrong. Maybe he wasn't absent because he didn't care, but because he didn't know. Maybe that's why Mom never let me inside her heart. My very existence was a constant reminder of all that she'd given up. I let it all sink in, realizing there was so much more I needed to know.

I refolded the letters and placed them back in my bag. My relationship with Mom had changed so much since I'd come home, and for that I was thankful. The letters shed light on things I had no idea about, and they forced me to view her through different eyes. For all the answers I'd found in the letters, there were just as many questions still unanswered. I finally knew who my father was, even if it was only the name Max. I would bide my time, and when the moment was right, I would ask her about him. It might be hard on her, but it was time I knew the truth.

Chapter Seventeen

The next few weeks passed by in a blur of fatigue and intense emotions. Helen and I took turns driving Mom to her twice-a-week chemo treatments. The medicine that was supposed to be clearing the cancer cells from her body had its share of side effects as well. I held her hair back while she vomited as the chemicals coursed through her frail body, until eventually there was no hair left to hold. Then I helped her wrap her bald head in a scarf and held her as she cried for all she'd lost.

I listened while she railed in anger, cursing God and anyone else who cared to listen for having to go through this personal hell. She vacillated between indignation and tears, and her mood could change quite abruptly. She yelled at me for the way I prepared her hot tea, then dissolved into tears and begged me to forgive her ungratefulness. She burst out laughing one day at something I said, but only minutes later I found her sobbing. She had trouble remembering most things, and would often walk into a room only to find she had no idea why she'd gone in there. I spent most days on the verge of tears myself, and I was thankful for the times Helen came to sit with her so I could regenerate.

My days consisted of keeping a watchful eye on her as she painfully made her way through each new obstacle of her illness; I was her companion and her nursemaid. There were good days and bad days; the bad ones made the good seem that much better. My mother grew to depend on me in a whole new way, and the situation, horrible as it was, brought us closer together.

Today was a good day, and I hummed a tune as I fixed us lunch, hopeful that I could coax some food into my mother's ever-shrinking body. I placed soup and sandwiches on the table and went down the hall to Mom's room to let her know it was ready. I found her looking through old photographs from when I was a baby, and the prodding in my heart told me it was time.

I'd put the information about Max on the back burner after I read the last of her letters. I was determined to broach the subject with her, but was waiting for the right moment. The moment couldn't get any more right than her looking at my baby pictures.

Sitting down on the bed beside her, I took the photo she handed me and looked at the curly, golden-blonde hair on my two-year-old head. I wasn't smiling in the picture; as a matter of fact, I had a very serious look on my tiny face. My eyes seemed sad and far too solemn for someone that young. Even at the tender age of two, they hinted of pain beyond my years.

"You were such a shy and worrisome little girl. But you always asked questions, even when you were just a wee thing." Mom chuckled and adjusted the handkerchief on her head, fingering it self-consciously.

"I guess there was a lot I wanted to know, even back then." I swallowed nervously, trying to work up the courage to say what I wanted to. "There's still a lot I want to know."

I looked Mom in the eye and instead of looking away as I'd expected, she held my gaze.

"I'm sure there is, Hope. There's a lot I never told you."

"Why, Mom? Why did you keep so many secrets from me?" My heart pumped quickly, nervous about the conversation we'd jumped into headfirst.

"Well, I'd like to say it was to protect you, but that would be a lie, I suppose. There was really nothing to protect you from. I know now it was really to protect me." She took a deep breath.

I'd returned the letters to their home in the attic a couple of weeks ago. I had the information I needed, but I wanted to see if Mom would tell me about Max without me having to ask.

"What did you need to be protected from?" I reached over and grabbed hold of her hand, which was ice cold. I knew this conversation was difficult for her, and I wanted to somehow help her through it.

"So many things." Mom dropped my hand and stood.

"I know this is hard for you, Mom."

"Stop being so nice to me. You should hate me for the things I did to you. You have every right! I was never the mother you needed me to be. But if you only knew why…." She began wringing her hands in frustration, and I suddenly wanted to stop the conversation. She was sick and weak. We didn't need to do this right now. I'd waited a lifetime to have this conversation, and I could certainly wait until she was feeling better.

"It's okay, Mom. Let's just forget it. Forget the whole thing. Let's talk about it all another day." I stood up and put my arm around her, trying to coax her into sitting down.

She agreed to sit, but refused to stop the conversation. "It's been too long already. It's time you knew the truth. About you, about me, about everything."

I couldn't believe this was real. I was finally going to learn the truth my mother worked nearly thirty years to conceal. But suddenly, I didn't want to know. I realized that once I knew, it would change everything. I would no longer be oblivious; I would have the information I'd so desperately wanted.

But once I did, I would have to do something with it. I wasn't ready, but in spite of my sudden reluctance, my mother began talking, unearthing a world of secrets.

"His name was Max, and he was my first love. We cared for each other so much, Hope. You think I don't know the way you felt about Sam, but I do. Oh, I know it so well. I loved him with a vengeance. He was my whole world. We made big plans. We were going to get married and escape this town. We would travel the world. He had a football scholarship, you see. He was an exquisite athlete. I had no doubt he could make the big time."

She didn't look at me, but instead stared off in the distance, as if she were reliving the memories while she shared them with me. I wanted to reach out and touch her, to connect with her somehow, but I didn't. I just listened, my heart thudding nervously as she told her story.

"Then, just a month before graduation, I found out about you and everything unraveled. Nothing could ever be the way we'd planned it. I knew Max would marry me. I didn't doubt that for a minute. He would want you. I knew he would do the right thing. But I couldn't see how destroying his future could ever be the right thing. There was only one path for me to choose." Mom turned and looked at me as tears streamed down her face. I wanted to ask so many questions, but I remained silent.

"I never told him why, Hope. I just broke things off with no explanation. The only way to make a clean break, the only way he would move on without me, was to hurt him. I refused his calls. I wouldn't speak to him. I know it broke his heart, but I guess he respected me enough not to push himself on me. I didn't tell him about you, Hope. God forgive me, I never told him he was a father. It was wrong, I know, but I didn't tell him."

Tears were running heavily down her face. As much as I knew I should be angry with her, in that moment, I couldn't be. She had been young and she had done what she thought was right at the time. Somehow I couldn't hold it against her anymore, not since I'd read the letters.

"It's okay, Mom. I know you think I'm mad at you, but I'm not. You've suffered enough." I put my arm around her, hoping she would believe the words I said.

She looked at me in amazement, and I could see the relief on her face. "How did I ever get lucky enough to have you for a daughter? Lord knows I don't deserve you. You should hate me for all the things I did to you. You have every right."

"I did hate you for a long time. But I don't anymore. We've both done it long enough, and I think it's time to move on, don't you?"

"You're amazing. I swear, I learn something new from you every day. Isn't it supposed to be the other way around? I'm supposed to teach you."

"I don't think there's really a right or a wrong way to do life, Mom. We're all just learning as we go." I patted her leg and took a breath, knowing what had to come next. "There is one thing you can do for me, though. I need to know who Max is. Please tell me about my father."

She took a deep breath, obviously having known I would ask the question eventually. She seemed to be wrestling with herself. She'd already told me a lot, but I needed to know this final, crucial secret. I had my suspicions about what she was going to say, but I needed to hear it from her.

"Max was my first love. He was a wonderful boy who grew into an amazing man. He did go away to college. He made good on his scholarship, and he was about to be drafted into the NFL when a knee injury changed it all. Instead, he finished college and moved back to Woodridge. He used his degree to open a business. He's lived here ever since." Mom looked at me as she spoke, perhaps waiting for me to piece things together.

"Please just tell me, Mom. Just say the words." I held my breath in anticipation, already knowing what was coming."

"Oh, Hope. I don't know how to tell you this. When he came back to town, you were almost five years old. My parents had moved to Hawaii by that time, and they gave me this house. I'd worked my way through nursing school, and I had a good job at the hospital. Max and I ran into each other right after he moved back, but when he saw you, I guess he just assumed I was involved with another man. I told him to stay away from me. By then I was angry at the world. Too angry to have any room in my heart for Max, or you for that matter. I should have told him that day, but I didn't. I knew I was a different person than the Maggie he loved. I was bitter. Time hadn't changed me for the better. I was afraid to tell him the truth. I was afraid he would reject me."

"This is a small town, Mom, and I don't know anyone named Max," I prodded.

Mom took a deep breath, preparing herself for this one final revelation. "Max was what he went by in school, but it's not his name. Hope, you've known him your whole life. Your father is Will Maxwell."

Chapter Eighteen

Mom's words hung in the air, and even though I'd already known in my gut what she was going to say, hearing her say it was still shocking. Will Maxwell, a man I had known most of my life, was my father. Until I read the letters, I hadn't pieced it all together, and I wondered if Will had ever wondered about me. It's a good thing I was already sitting, because my legs would no longer have supported me. It all made sense to me, the fact that Will and I had been unlikely friends. Even though neither of us knew our real connection, we'd somehow still had an impact upon each other.

It also made sense why he always asked me about Mom, and why he'd been so upset to learn about her illness. After reading the letters and knowing that he was Max, I understood how deeply the two of them loved one another. Will had never married either; perhaps that was because he never got over Mom. There were so many thoughts inside my head, and the walls of Mom's bedroom began closing in on me. I felt claustrophobic and I had to get out of there.

"I need some air. This is a lot for me to take in. I'll be back in a while." I squeezed her hand and left the room before she could say anything else.

I wasn't angry with her, but I needed to be alone to process everything she'd just told me. I had to be away from her in order to do that. I grabbed the car keys as I left the house, jumped inside my mother's car, and drove with no real destination in mind as I mulled over the information about my father.

If I'd thought my life was complicated before, that was nothing compared to how I felt now. What was I supposed to do with the knowledge that Will Maxwell was my father? I didn't even know how I felt about it. I was happy, in a way, but more confused than ever. He was an amazing, kind, gentle man, and if I could handpick someone to be my father, I'd choose him in a second.

But what did that mean, exactly? I wouldn't be the only person affected by my decision. Will had spent his whole life unattached. What would he do if I suddenly waltzed into Maxwell's Grocery and said, "Hey, guess what, Dad? It's me, the daughter you never knew you had!" Would he be happy or would he wish he'd never found out?

I thought of Will and his golden-blond crew cut, suddenly realizing his hair was the exact color of my own. His chocolate-brown eyes, always full of laughter, were mirror images of mine as well. Had we both been so blind that we'd never noticed these similarities before? I'd obviously inherited his physical traits, and I wondered what other characteristics he'd passed on to me through the gene pool.

I knew him, but not well. I didn't know what he liked, or what he hated. I had no idea how he drank his coffee, or if he even liked coffee. I didn't know the real him, just as he had no idea who I really was. The only thing I knew for sure was that he was a good man, and he was my dad. Being able to put a face to the lifelong mystery image of my father was satisfying, but it was also terrifying.

I was forced to rethink everything I'd ever believed about the kind of man my father was. I'd certainly never had a high opinion of the person I believed abandoned my mother and me. I'd been angry at him for all of my life. Knowing that man was Will, and understanding that he might have no idea I was his child changed everything. I felt sorry for him, and for myself, when I thought about all the time we'd lost with each other. But I also felt sorry for Mom, knowing she'd given up the love of her life in the belief that she was doing the right thing for him.

I drove around a while longer and thought about each and every encounter I'd had with Will throughout my life. I finally came to the conclusion that the only option was to tell him the truth. He would be shocked, for sure, and he would probably be angry with Mom for her deception. But once he got past that, the Will I knew would accept it. He hadn't done anything wrong, and he deserved to finally know the truth. Twenty-eight years was too long to be oblivious to the details of your own life. No one knew that better than I did.

It was dark when I finally pulled into the driveway. The lights were off in the house, and I knew Mom was probably in bed. I quietly went inside and found her sleeping. She was clutching a photo of me taken in the hospital the day I was born. My heart expanded with love. I realized how emotional the day I was born must have been for her. She'd just given birth, without any support at all. She was facing a lifetime of parenting alone. I'd never given her any credit for doing it all without anyone's help. She must have been scared to death.

I leaned down and kissed her gently on her bald head. She'd removed the handkerchief, and her scalp felt smooth under my lips. As I watched her sleep, I knew for certain that there was no anger left inside me for my mother. I'd used it all up; it was gone. All that remained was compassion and love.

Her life had been hard, and she'd experienced very little happiness. As sorry as I was that she was sick, I believed with everything in me that it was all for a reason. If she hadn't gotten cancer, I'd have never come back home. Mom and I were getting a second chance to find happiness and peace. We'd wasted a lot of years, but it seemed like we still had time to make it right.

I quietly crept up the creaky stairs to my bedroom. It had been a long, exhausting day and I was tired, but I longed for the peacefulness of my hideaway on the roof. Grabbing my favorite blanket, I lifted the squeaky window and carefully crawled outside. I was still afraid of falling, but I reminded myself how much I loved it out there. I steadied myself on the slope of the roof and sat down. It was cold, so I pulled the blanket over my legs and zipped up my jacket.

In the distance, I heard the crashing of the waves and closed my eyes. I let the tranquility of my surroundings settle over me, thinking of how much I'd changed since coming back to Woodridge. I wasn't the same person who'd arrived a few months ago. There were still things that I wished were different, but I felt like I was growing a little bit stronger every day.

The fragments of the woman I used to be were slowly coming together to form a new me. I was still getting to know this new me, but I had to admit that I liked her. I'd forgiven Mom, I was helping her fight for her life, I was writing again, and I finally knew who my father was. I was less and less the scared, insecure, broken woman I'd been when I arrived.

Things were far from perfect, but I was handling it. I still had to finalize my divorce and figure out a way to coexist with Sam and his family living next door, both of which would take superhuman amounts of strength. But I was learning to take it all in stride. My anxiety, although still very much a monster I hadn't yet conquered, was no longer paralyzing. I'd made it through all the turmoil of the past few months without medication, even though I still kept the bottle close by just in case. Admittedly, I was terrified about my talk with Will, but somehow I knew I would get through that, too.

I was congratulating myself on how mature I'd become when I heard the oh-so-familiar sound of a creaking window and saw Sam crawl onto the rooftop next door. I rolled my eyes, finding it ironic that just when I thought things were looking up, I was proven wrong. My life was a series of two baby steps forward and one gargantuan fall back.

Sam glanced in my direction and seemed surprised to see me. It gave me an odd sense of satisfaction knowing that he still went out on his roof, even after all these years. It was our special thing, and I was happy to know he was still connected to me in that small way.

But then I remembered that his life no longer had anything to do with me. For all I knew, it was his special thing with Annie now. That was something I didn't want to see, so I collected my things and stood up to go inside before she joined him.

"Hope," Sam said quietly. It sounded more like a question than a greeting.

"Good night, Sam." I briefly met his eyes before I turned away. I was astonished at the pain and turmoil I saw there.

I needed to go before I lost control, so I slid back inside. As I closed the window and adjusted the lace curtains over it, I saw that Sam was still looking helplessly in my direction. I was flooded with sadness as I climbed into bed and closed my eyes in a lame attempt to block him out.

Chapter Nineteen

Walking along the beach the next morning, I marveled as my footprints were washed away by an incoming wave, amazed at the vast beauty all around me. Beginning each day beside the ocean was a habit of mine these days, and it had a calming effect on my frazzled nerves. I basked in the solitude, reveling in the fact that there wasn't another person for miles around this morning.

Checking my phone for about the hundredth time since I'd awakened, I looked to see if there was a new text from Kelsey. She'd left Seattle an hour ago to make the two-hour drive to Woodridge, and she would be staying with me for three glorious days. I couldn't wait. We hadn't seen each other since she flew to New York last year for a visit, and the anticipation was killing me.

Kelsey's visit was coming at the perfect time. Even though I was growing emotionally stronger every day, I was still so close to the edge that I often feared another stressful event might just send me toppling over. Her presence grounded me; she was my rock.

My phone buzzed.

Kelsey: I had to stop and stretch. Don't panic. I'll be there in a little over an hour.

I decided I should head back home and shower, so I didn't look as if I'd just crawled out of bed when she arrived.

I made my way down the path, the thick fog hanging in the air like a blanket and reducing my visibility. In the distance, I heard voices, but the conversation was drowned out by the roar of the ocean behind me. As the voices drew closer, my heart thudded in recognition. It was Sam and Bridget, and I was unable to escape.

"Hope!" Bridget ran to me and threw her little arms around my waist, hugging me tightly. I hadn't seen her in weeks, and from the excited look on her face, she was happy to see me. "Oh, I've missed you so much. I haven't seen you in so long!"

"Hey, Bridget, I've missed you too. I've been really busy helping my mom. How are you?" I swallowed, feeling like I'd suddenly eaten a mouthful of sand as Sam's handsome face came into view.

"Hello, Hope. It's good to see you again." He looked hesitantly at me.

"Sam. I hope you're doing well." My voice sounded so formal, but it was the only way to control the urge I had to throw myself into his arms.

"Yeah, I'm doing all right." He shrugged and smiled, but his face held such sadness. I wondered if being this close was as hard for him as it was for me.

"Bridget's missed seeing you." He put his arm protectively around his daughter as he spoke, as if to shield her from the pain I'd caused by my absence. I felt horrible for disappointing Bridget.

"I know, and I've missed her too. It's been hard.... Mom's having a rough time with her chemo and it seems my days just fly by." It was the truth, but I also knew it was a convenient lie.

"It sounds like maybe you need a break. How about you come over for dinner tonight? It will be good to catch up, and Bridget will be thrilled to have some time with you." Sam's eyes locked on to mine. The depth of feeling nearly knocked me off my feet.

"Yes! Please, please, please, Hope? Come over for dinner!" Bridget hugged me again tightly as she jumped up and down and begged. When her little blue eyes looked up at me, I had no idea how I could refuse.

I wanted to run, hide; anything I could do to get away from Sam. I would rather eat nails than sit painfully through family dinner at his house. I couldn't sit across from Annie, in the home she'd made with my Sam, and politely say "please pass the potatoes." As much as I wanted to be mature about the whole thing, what I really wanted to do was throw the potatoes in her face. I knew I'd made the mistake of letting Sam go, but an irrational part of me still held her partially responsible. No, thank you. That was not an experience I intended to have anytime soon.

"I'm sorry. I really can't. Kelsey will be arriving this afternoon to spend a few days with me." I smiled benignly, happy I had a legitimate reason to say no.

"Kelsey? I haven't seen her in years. It would be great to catch up with her, too. Bring her along. Both of you come over." Sam's enthusiasm was annoyingly cute and hard to ignore. He was trying very hard to convince me. Maybe it was time to finally make amends with Annie and Sam and accept their relationship. I'd done a lot of hard things since I'd come back home, but I didn't know if I could do that.

"Come on, Hope. I miss you. I want to show you my room. We just painted it. Come have dinner with us." Bridget gave me her imploring, puppy-dog eyes and I melted.

It was impossible for me to say no to that girl. I didn't want to hurt her, and since they'd also invited Kelsey, I no longer had a convenient excuse. My resolve began to crumble.

"Well, I suppose we can…." I couldn't believe I'd just agreed, but when Bridget's face lit up with excitement, I knew I had to go through with it. There was no backing out now.

"Perfect. We'll see you around seven o'clock, then. Come on, Bridget. Let's see what treasures the ocean washed up for us this morning." Sam grabbed his daughter's hand, and they continued on the path toward the beach while I trudged home, kicking myself for not shouting an emphatic no to their invitation.

What was I thinking, agreeing to dinner with Annie and

Sam? It was a disaster just waiting to happen. How in the world was I going to smile politely while they cozied up to each other at the dinner table? I would either say something horrible or run away in tears. Either option didn't sit well with me.

The only silver lining to that dark cloud was at least Kelsey would be with me. She could be a buffer between me and the happy couple. I wondered how upset Annie would be when Sam went home and told her he'd invited us to dinner. I couldn't imagine she'd be pleased about the situation. We'd never gotten along, even before everything that happened between her and Sam.

I sighed as I went inside to shower. Kelsey would arrive soon, and I was looking forward to that, even if I had just signed my death warrant by agreeing to dinner at Sam's house.

Mom was resting and Kelsey and I had just finished lunch. Our empty plates sat on the table beside us as we lounged on the porch swing. I couldn't believe she was here, sitting beside me on my porch, just as we'd done a million times when we were young.

"I'm glad you're here, Kel. I've missed you so much." I squeezed my best friend's hand.

"Me too, sweetie. Daniel and the boys were sorry they couldn't come too. Personally, I'm happy to be getting a little time away from them. I'm selfish, and I want all of your attention. I refuse to share the next three days with anyone."

She laughed, her wild, contagious belly laugh, and I couldn't help but join in. She had that effect on people.

"So much has happened since I came back. I feel like I'm about a hundred years older, but it's been good, too. I have important news to tell you."

"Have you seen Sam again?"

"I did a nice job of avoiding him for the last couple of weeks, but that came to a crashing halt this morning. I ran into him and his daughter, Bridget, on the beach. They invited us over for dinner tonight."

"You said no, right?"

"Of course I said no." I rolled my eyes, wishing that was the end of it. "But then Bridget begged me to come, and I sort of said yes. You're invited too. Say you'll go with me. I can't go alone."

"Hope, I cannot believe you agreed to this. You're out of your mind. You're going to sit down to dinner with Annie? You're going to watch the love of your life in his house with his wife? You're just a glutton for punishment, aren't you?" Kelsey shook her head at me, but she had a knowing smile on her face.

"It was because of Bridget. She's such a sweetheart. I can't say no to her! Just wait until you meet her. You'll see. She's like a miniature version of Sam, and she melts my heart. Besides, I'm more than a little curious about the situation with Annie. I've been home for months and I have yet to see her. It's weird. Bridget's never mentioned her. She totally clammed up the one time I asked her about her mom. It's like Annie's a ghost or something. I need to find out what's going on."

"Sucker." Kelsey giggled at me. "Of course I'll go. I wouldn't send you to the guillotine all by yourself. I'll be there to watch it all go down, and I'll pick up your head after it rolls."

"Thanks a lot." I couldn't help but laugh.

"And we will spend all afternoon getting ready. You have to be drop-dead gorgeous when Annie lays eyes on you after all these years."

"I love you, Kel. It's like you read my mind." I was so glad she was here. "There's more, too. I know who my dad is."

"What? Are you trying to give me a heart attack? How can you be so casual about it? How did you find out?"

"I found an old box of letters up in the attic. They were from Mom's first love. Long story short, I read them all and found out that this mystery man named Max is my father. I asked her about it, and she told me the truth. You're never going to guess who it is. Not in a million years."

"Who? Tell me."

"Will Maxwell."

"You're kidding. He's your father?" Kelsey looked at me for a minute before she continued. "Come to think of it, you do look a lot like him. Weird."

"I know, right? I thought the exact same thing after I found out. You know, Will and Mom loved each other so much when they were young. It's a shame they never ended up together."

"Well, neither of them ever got married. Maybe they're still in love."

"No, I can't imagine that after all these years."

"Are you kidding me? You of all people should know that it's entirely possible. Look at how you still feel about Sam."

"Maybe you're right. I never really thought of that. You know, Mom and I are more alike than I ever knew. She's changed so much. I really want some happiness for her."

"She's certainly due for some. And so are you."

"I think she's far more likely to get her happy ending than I am. After all, the love of my life has his own family."

"Speaking of the love of your life, let's go upstairs and decide what you're going to wear to dinner tonight. It needs to be something that makes Sam regret losing you, and makes Annie green with envy."

Kelsey grabbed my hand and dragged me inside.

Chapter Twenty

Looking at myself in the mirror, I couldn't believe what I saw. Kelsey was a magician. She'd rummaged through my closet until she found sleek black jeans, which she'd paired with a low-cut red silk blouse. Black boots, a chunky silver necklace, and silver bangle bracelets completed the look. I'd been living in yoga pants and sweatshirts, so I felt a bit out of my element.

Kelsey used the flat iron on my long, wavy hair, and the result was impressive. My honey-colored tresses were silky, smooth, and shiny. She'd also expertly applied my makeup, and the completed look took me by surprise.

"You, my dear, are stunning." Kelsey stepped back and surveyed me from across the room. She let out a whistle, and I couldn't help but laugh.

"I have to agree with you, Kel. I look pretty darn good, thanks to you."

"It was a piece of cake. You're gorgeous to begin with,

so I really couldn't go wrong. Sam is going to have to pick his jaw up off the floor when he sees you. Annie is going to wish she was you."

"I shouldn't be so worried about impressing him, but I am. It's so wrong to feel that way about someone else's husband, but he was mine first. He should be married to me right now, and he would be if I hadn't been such an idiot." I blew out a frustrated breath. "I'm nervous. I hope I don't make a fool of myself tonight. I've been kicking myself all afternoon for agreeing to this."

"Your best bet is to say as little as possible. You should let me direct the conversation, that way you won't say something embarrassing to Annie or Sam." Kelsey hooked the strap on her shoe and informed me she was ready to go. "Just smile and nod. You can't go wrong with that."

Kelsey and I made sure Mom was settled in front of the television, giving her strict instructions to call us immediately if she needed anything. As I leaned down to kiss her good-bye, Mom patted my cheek and said, "Good luck, honey. I'm sure tonight is going to turn out just fine. You'll see."

"Nothing good can possibly come out of tonight. It was a mistake for me to agree to this." I smiled nervously at her.

We hadn't talked any more about my feelings for Sam, but she knew how much he meant to me. Come to think of it, she'd never mentioned Annie either. It was all very strange. She had an unusual, serene look on her face this evening, like she knew something she wasn't telling me. I wondered what it meant. She really seemed sure that things were going to go better than I thought they would at dinner, but I had a hard time believing it would be anything less than disastrous.

I took a deep breath as Kelsey rang Sam's doorbell. Flashbacks ran through my mind of that horrible day Sam had told me Annie was pregnant. It was the worst day of my life, and I was about to see the result of it played out before my eyes. My mom was crazy to think this could ever turn out well.

Bridget answered the door, and she looked adorable in her yellow-and-white polka-dot dress and Mary Janes. I reminded myself that I was doing this for her. She was the only reason I was going through with this. I'd never seen her in a dress before, and I thought it was sweet that she'd put one on for me.

"Bridget, this is my best friend, Kelsey." I introduced the two and noticed that Bridget seemed shy with Kelsey. Funny, she'd never been that way when we met. I remembered June telling me that it was rare for her to feel comfortable with strangers.

"Nice to meet you, Bridget. I have four little boys, so being around a pretty girl like you is a breath of fresh air. I'll bet you won't put any frogs on my seat at the dinner table, will you?" Kelsey laughed and Bridget gasped.

"Do your sons really do that to you?" Bridget asked with wide eyes.

"Oh, honey, they do that and more. But I love them anyhow." I could tell that as soon as the shyness wore off, the two of them would get along just fine.

Just then, Sam joined us at the front door and my heart

nearly stopped. He certainly cleaned up nicely in his khaki pants and navy button-up shirt that brought out the blue of his eyes. He smelled like soap and aftershave, and the scent was intoxicating. His blond hair looked as if he'd spent extra time styling it, but it still had that slightly wild, rumpled look I loved. My fingers itched to reach out and tangle into it, so I stuffed my hands in my pockets to resist the urge.

"Hope, you look amazing." When he said my name, I felt like the world stopped turning on its axis. Sam gave me tunnel vision; I couldn't see anything but him when he was in the room. Somewhere in the recesses of my mind I knew he'd paid me a compliment and I should thank him, but I was incapable of speech. Thankfully, Kelsey came to my rescue.

"Sam, it's so great to see you. It's been too long! Thanks for having us over." Kelsey and Sam embraced, exchanged pleasantries, and gave me a chance to regain my composure.

I congratulated myself on not passing out. So far, I was doing all right, but I hadn't yet seen Annie. That would be the real test of my fortitude. Sam and Bridget led us into the living room where we all sat down.

"Dinner should be ready in a few minutes. I made clam linguine." Sam looked right at me as he spoke the words.

"Clam linguine—my favorite. You remembered." I couldn't believe he'd gone to the trouble of making my favorite meal.

"Of course I remembered. I haven't forgotten a thing." His words hung in air that suddenly seemed charged with electricity. I cleared my throat and tried to think of something to say in response, but nothing came to me.

Instead, I took in my surroundings. It was a lived-in room, not fancy, but neat. The black leather couches and black-and-white photographs of nautical scenes spoke of Sam's taste. I wondered if Annie had the same decorating preferences, because so far I saw nothing to indicate a feminine presence in the house. Photographs of Sam and Bridget through the years adorned the walls, but I noticed that Annie was not in any of them. I'd known for a while that something was wrong. Where was Annie? What had happened between the two of them after I left town? An uncomfortable gnawing began in my stomach.

"Kelsey, would you like to come see my bedroom? Daddy and I just painted it purple. That's my favorite color." Bridget spoke quietly.

"I'd love to, honey. I'll bet you keep it neat as a pin, too. Oh, the differences between little boys and little girls. Let's go." Kelsey allowed herself to be led upstairs by Bridget, leaving Sam and me in the room alone. It was awkward, to say the least.

I cleared my throat twice. "Can I help you with dinner?" I hoped he would say yes, so I'd have something to occupy myself with.

"Sure, let's go." Following Sam down the hallway toward the kitchen, I noticed more photographs of Sam and Bridget, but still none of Annie. Now I knew for certain that something was wrong. There wasn't a trace of her in the house.

Sam went to the counter and began slicing up a French baguette. One glance around the room told me he had dinner completely under control. It was obvious that he didn't need my help at all. Bridget and Kelsey were still upstairs, and I was more confused than ever about why I hadn't seen Annie. I decided to just ask the dreaded question.

"Sam, where's Annie?" I didn't sugarcoat my words, but instead went straight to the point.

"I'm not sure what you mean." He laid the knife down on the cutting board and walked across the room to where I was standing, confusion on his face.

"Annie. Your wife. Bridget's mother." It was frustrating that he was making me explain the obvious.

"Annie…." Sam raked his hands through his hair in a nervous gesture I recognized from when he was a teenager. "Hope, Annie's dead."

The words fell like a lead balloon in the room. Nothing could have surprised me more. Annie was dead? I didn't understand. Annie was only twenty-eight years old, the same age as me. How could she be dead? It didn't make any sense.

"I… I… am sorry… I don't understand," I stammered, looking helplessly at Sam.

"Annie has been dead for ten years, Hope. She died giving birth to Bridget." Sam spoke matter-of-factly, obviously surprised that I didn't know.

"I need to sit down." My knees buckled as I collapsed onto a barstool.

"I just thought you knew. I didn't realize… you thought…." Sam seemed to be as much at a loss for words as I was.

"I didn't know. How could I? No one ever told me anything about you. I thought you and Annie got married after graduation and lived happily ever after somewhere. I didn't know you were right here or that she was… dead." It was difficult for me to say the word.

I suddenly felt awful for every mean thought I'd ever had about Annie. I'd disliked her for so long, never realizing that she lost her life at such a young age. No one deserved that. Poor Bridget had grown up without a mother. No wonder she didn't want to talk about it when I asked her. She'd never even known her at all. And Sam had the responsibility of raising the little girl alone. Thankfully they had June; sweet June, who'd lost her daughter so young. This was what Mom had been trying to tell me.

I was a horrible person. Here I'd been wishing that Annie was old and ugly and she'd never even made it past the age of eighteen. I'd dressed up hoping to make her jealous of me, and she was dead.

"I'm sorry this is such a shock to you. I honestly thought you knew. Is that why you've been avoiding me? Because you thought I was married to Annie?"

"Well, yeah. I knew I couldn't bear to see the two of you together, happily married." I rose from the stool, feeling like I needed to run, but knowing I had to hear the story.

"Hope." Sam pulled me toward him.

He was only inches away and everything inside me screamed to reach out and touch him. Tentatively, I lifted my hand and caressed his cheek. I'd loved this man for as long as I could remember. I'd wished every day that we could be together, and now there was nothing standing between us.

Ever so slowly, Sam's face drew closer to mine, and I

inhaled his achingly familiar scent. He put his arm around me, pulling me to him. Placing both of his hands on my face, he lowered his lips to mine. It was a whisper of a kiss that quickly caught fire.

On instinct, I tangled my fingers into Sam's hair, holding on for dear life, just as I'd done hundreds of times when we were young. He backed me up until we ran into the counter, but still we didn't stop. I tasted him; I drank him in like a woman who was finally feasting after a famine. Time stopped and nothing in the world mattered except his lips on mine. I didn't let go; I never wanted to let go of him again.

"Something is certainly cooking in this kitchen." Kelsey's voice from the doorway sent us both crashing back to reality. I pulled away from Sam, smoothing my clothing and hair self-consciously.

I was mortified that his daughter had just seen us kissing. Sam, on the other hand, had a mile-wide grin on his face. He didn't look embarrassed in the least. Bridget smiled happily at her father and gave me her all-knowing look. I was beginning to think the two of them were conspiring against me.

"Um, yeah, dinner is ready, ladies. Let's eat." Sam led us into the dining room.

There was no possible way I could eat, not after what just happened. But I remembered that he had worked hard to make my favorite meal, and I knew I had to try. It would be rude not to eat what he'd prepared specifically for me.

I took a few bites of the clam linguine, which tasted delicious. Sam was an excellent cook, but he always had been.

I wasn't in the mood for conversation, and was thankful that Kelsey kept up a steady stream of chatter throughout the meal. She kept us entertained with stories of her sons' shenanigans, asked Bridget questions about school, and reminisced with Sam.

Kelsey kept glancing my way, certainly as confused as I had been about Annie's mysterious absence, but she didn't bring it up. She would be shocked when I told her the story. Throughout dinner I said very little, but my mind roared loudly.

Sam kept looking at me, trying to meet my eyes. I was still reeling from our kiss in his kitchen. If Kelsey and Bridget hadn't come in, I'm sure we would have done more than just kiss. That was the very last thing I'd ever imagined would happen tonight. I did my best to avoid looking at him, knowing how transparent I was. He'd always been able to read my thoughts, and right now I didn't want him to.

I was so confused about everything I'd learned tonight. I still loved him; that was a given. From the kiss we'd shared, I gathered he still felt something for me. For the last ten years, Annie had been the obstacle standing in the way of Sam and me being together, but now I knew that was no longer the case. Jonathan wasn't an obstacle either. At least, he wouldn't be as soon as I convinced him to sign the divorce papers.

Nothing at all was standing in the way of Sam and me being together. Instead of making me happy, though, the reality terrified me. I'd always heard the saying, "Be careful what you wish for. You just might get it." I never truly understood its meaning until that very moment.

We finished dinner, and after Sam's refusal to let us help him clean up, Kelsey and I decided it was time to go. I needed to get away from him, so I could clear my head and figure out what on earth I was going to do. I also needed to tell Kelsey what I'd found out about Annie. I was counting on her levelheadedness to help me put it all into perspective.

Sam and Bridget walked us outside. Bridget asked Kelsey if she wanted to see her tree house and the pair took off, leaving the two of us alone once again. Now I knew for sure that Bridget was plotting to get her dad alone with me. If I hadn't been so conflicted, I would have thought it was pretty cute.

My phone buzzed loudly inside my purse, and I checked it immediately, worried it might be Mom. It wasn't; instead, it was Jonathan. I clicked Decline and sent him straight to voice mail. The man just refused to give up. He was the last person I wanted to deal with tonight.

"I'm glad you came over." Sam put his hand on my arm, and that simple touch felt so intimate. The pull between the two of us was magnetic, and ten years apart had done nothing to diminish its power. It took every ounce of strength I had not to give in again.

"Thank you for dinner. It was delicious. You always were such a great cook. It was sweet of you to make my favorite meal."

"You know I'd do anything for you. I know the news about Annie was a shock. That was a rotten way for you to find out."

"Yeah, I'm still trying to wrap my brain around it, I think. I didn't say it before, but I'm really sorry for your loss, Sam. That must have been hard on you."

"The whole situation was hard. You know better than anyone that things with me and Annie were anything but ideal. She loved me and I loved you. It was bound to fail, but we wanted to do the right thing for our daughter. Annie didn't deserve to die so young. It's been really hard for Bridget, growing up without a mother. I do my best, but I don't know how to be a mom." The sadness on his face twisted my heart.

"You're a great father, Sam. That's obvious. Bridget is a lucky little girl to have you."

"I'm the lucky one." He cleared his throat, and I could tell he wasn't finished talking. "I just want you to know I'm so sorry I hurt you all those years ago. It killed me to know what I did to you. The guilt is something I've lived with every day for the last ten years."

"Honestly, as much as I blamed you, it was my fault. I pushed you away. I accused you of something you'd never even done. I guess it was all meant to be, though, because look at what came out of it. You got Bridget."

"Yeah, she's amazing. But a big part of me can't help but wish things were different. I'd never give up having her, but I wish I hadn't hurt you in the process." He traced my cheek with his fingertip.

"I've wished every single day that things were different, but they aren't. I think we both need to accept that." Tears stung my eyes and I tried to blink them back, but they fell anyway.

He leaned toward me and I knew he was going to kiss me again. As much as I wanted it, I couldn't let it happen. There were too many things I had to sort out in my heart, and kissing him again would just complicate it. Besides, I was still hurt over what happened with Annie, and I didn't know if I could ever get past that. I was so afraid to trust my feelings for Sam again. I was terrified of being hurt if I did. Kissing him earlier had been a mistake, but it was one I couldn't make again. I needed to be strong. I had enough on my plate right now, and jumping into a relationship that had the potential to completely destroy me if it didn't work out was too big of a risk.

Despite my best efforts, Sam pulled me closer to him. My body betrayed me, and I let him. He leaned into me and gently pushed my hair away from my ear. I tingled from head to toe as I felt his hot breath on my neck. He inhaled deeply, and just when I thought he was going to kiss me again, he instead placed his lips to my ear and said, "I'll love you forever, Hope. You and me against the world, remember?"

My knees went weak and my tummy flipped. He'd said those exact words to me a million times, but I'd never dreamed I would hear them again. It seemed to be everything I wanted, but somehow I just couldn't let go of the past. "Sam… I can't…. I have to go." I reluctantly tore myself away from him, although my body ached to do the opposite.

I called good-bye to Bridget and began walking home. I glanced back briefly and he was just standing there, looking as if he'd lost his best friend. I wanted to turn around and run back into his arms. I wanted to tell him that nothing mattered except the way we still felt about each other. As much as I wanted to, though, I didn't. I just kept walking away from him. Kelsey strode briskly to catch up to me.

"What gives, Hope? What's going on?" Kelsey looked at me, confusion written all over her face.

I led her to the porch swing where we both sat. "Annie's dead, Kel." The words were difficult to say, but I didn't have the energy to do anything except blurt them out.

"What? When? I know I lost touch with Woodridge after my parents and I moved away, but I would have thought we would have heard about that." Kelsey's face crinkled.

"I don't understand either. I think Mom tried to tell me a couple of times, but I never listened. It's like Annie's death was just swept under the rug. I'm sure June must have been devastated, and I can't imagine what Sam went through as a single dad." I sighed.

"What am I going to do? I still love him, and he made it clear that he feels the same way about me. What do I do with that?"

"What do you want to do? The answer seems pretty obvious."

"I don't know what I want, and the answer is anything but obvious to me. I want Sam. I want things to be the way they were before he slept with Annie. But I can't have that, can I? I don't know if I'll ever be able to get past that. I want to, but I'm not sure I can. What if we try again and I lose him a second time? I don't think I could take that."

"It's a lot to digest for one night, sweetie. Let's get some rest. Things will look better in the morning."

As I lay in bed with darkness settling in all around me, I was more confused than ever. I loved Sam so much, and kissing him tonight felt like coming home. Nothing was standing between us any more except my feelings, but that seemed like a huge crevasse I could never cross. It was easier to be angry with him, however irrational that anger was. It was easier to long for something I couldn't have. It was easier to mourn for all that we'd lost. The hard part was allowing myself to be vulnerable again, and as much as I wanted to, I didn't know if I could do that.

Chapter Twenty-One

"Kelsey, Mom will tell you exactly where to go once you get to the hospital. She knows the drill pretty well by now." I closed the car door for Mom as I gave Kelsey last-minute instructions. She'd offered to drive Mom to her chemo treatment this morning, so I would have some free time to visit Will.

"We will be just fine, sweetie. Don't worry. Are you sure you want to do this?" Mom looked at me through her rolled-down window. I'd told her last night that I was going to talk to Will today. She was certain he would hate her once he knew. She confided in me that she'd wanted to tell him a long time ago, but she'd lost her nerve. I knew she was worried about the outcome, but she'd also told me it was my choice.

"It's time to get it all out in the open. See you guys in a bit." Kelsey smiled supportively at me as they pulled out of the driveway. She was the one who had encouraged me to do it today, and to not let it go on any longer. I told her I couldn't because I had to take Mom to treatment. She explained she was driving Mom, leaving me with no more excuses.

I hopped into the green Honda I'd recently purchased for myself and drove toward Maxwell's. I had a queasy feeling, which had been there since last night when I made the decision to talk to him. I knew that telling him was the right thing to do, but I was terrified. I honestly had no idea how he would react to the news.

Would he be angry with me? Would he hate Mom for deceiving him? I didn't want either of those things to happen, but I knew I couldn't control his reaction. The only thing I could do was tell him the truth and see what happened. The worst-case scenario was that he wouldn't want to be part of my life, and I reasoned that I'd gone this long without a father, so I could handle that.

I pulled into the parking lot, grabbed my purse, and went inside. Will stood next to the cash register, chatting animatedly with one of his employees. I was terrified and wanted to jump back in my car and forget the whole thing. Perhaps I should have taken one of the anxiety pills today, but it was too late for that now.

I would face this hurdle just as I'd done everything else—without medication. Kelsey said that I needed to bolster my courage with positive self-talk, so I'd been telling myself how strong and capable I was. Although I doubted anything could make this moment easier, I took a deep breath and approached my father.

"Hello." I cleared my throat and he looked up and saw me standing there.

"Hope. It's great to see you. How's your mom?" I smiled,

thinking of how many times we'd exchanged these exact words over my lifetime. The number was too high to count.

"She's doing as well as can be expected, I guess. The treatments are hard on her. Dr. Riddles says she's exactly where she should be at this point, but I won't lie, it's been rough."

"I'm sorry you're both going through this. It's hard on your mother, but it has to be hard on you, too."

"Yes, it has been." I knew I was stalling, and I decided I should just dive right in with the reason I was there. It was best to do it quickly, before I lost my nerve. "I need to talk to you. Is there somewhere private we can do that?"

"Sure, but you're making me a little nervous." He chuckled, but there was no denying the worried expression on his face.

"I don't mean to. But I do need to talk to you. It's important."

"Okay, let's go back to my office. No one will bother us there." He led me through the store and into his office, shutting the door behind us.

I glanced around the room, curious about the place where my father spent so much of his time. It was neat, but not compulsively so. Papers were stacked on his glass-topped desk, but there seemed to be some organization to the piles. The screen saver on his computer was a photo of him holding a salmon the length of his arm. I'd forgotten that he was a fisherman. That was something he and Sam had in common.

"So, what did you need to talk to me about?" Will motioned to the leather chair in front of his desk, and he sat down in the swiveling one behind it.

I looked across the desk at my father, and for the life of me, I had no idea how to start the conversation I'd come to have. While I considered my words, I couldn't help but notice the similarities between the two of us. We sat in our chairs in identical fashion, with right leg crossed over left, and hands folded neatly in our laps. His hands, although much larger, were shaped exactly like my own, with long, slender fingers. There was no mistaking that our unique golden-blond hair color or our chocolate-brown eyes were mirror images of one another. I wondered why it had taken almost thirty years for me to notice these similarities.

"First of all, Mom knows I'm here." I cleared my throat, which felt like it was coated in cotton balls, and began. "This is not easy to say. In fact, I've rehearsed the whole thing in my mind over and over, and I still don't know the right words. I guess I'll just say it—I know that you were in love with my mother."

"Yes, I was. Maggie meant the world to me. The day I lost her was the worst day of my life." His gaze didn't waver from my own. He didn't flinch or deny it. I didn't know what I'd expected, but blatant honesty wasn't it.

"I want to understand. If you loved her so much, why didn't you keep trying to win her back?"

"Loving someone means respecting them, and Maggie made it very clear that her feelings for me had changed. I respected her enough to keep my distance, even though it wasn't what I wanted." Will uncrossed his legs and wiped his hands across his pants. I wondered if his palms were sweating as much as mine.

"Can you tell me your side of what happened after the breakup?"

"There's not much to tell. I had a scholarship, so I went away to college. I would have given it up in a second to stay here with Maggie if she'd given me any indication that's what she wanted. But she didn't. She wouldn't even speak to me. Just a month before we graduated, she broke things off with no explanation. I was a football player, and I had big dreams of being drafted into the NFL. Part of me thought that was the way to win back Maggie's heart. If I really made something of myself, maybe she'd want me again."

"Do you honestly believe that?"

"I don't know what I believe. What I know to be true is that Maggie moved on." Will shifted in his chair and averted his eyes from mine for the first time since the conversation started. "I didn't get drafted. It almost happened, but I injured my knee and that was the end of my football dreams. So I decided to come home. I thought that maybe Maggie and I could start over again. I hoped that some time apart had made her realize she loved me as much as I loved her."

Will stood and began pacing. There were a million questions I wanted to ask, but I just let him talk instead.

"When I came back, the first thing on my mind was contacting Maggie. It had been five years since I'd heard anything about her, and I honestly didn't know what to expect. I didn't even know for sure if she was still in Woodridge." He stopped pacing and turned to look at me. "The first day I was back in town, I ran into her at the gas station, of all places.

She had changed, that much was obvious. There was nothing at all left of the happy, carefree girl I'd left behind."

I shifted in my chair, knowing that this would be the hardest part for him to tell and for me to hear. I also knew I was about to change his entire life with the revelation that I was his child.

Will continued. "I almost didn't recognize her. She'd cut off all her lovely auburn hair and was thinner than I'd ever seen her. Her blue eyes were no longer full of laughter. They looked hollow and cold. The change in my Maggie was so drastic that I didn't even know what to say to her. It was obvious that she wasn't happy, which made me even more determined to win her back."

"What happened next?" I was literally on the edge of my seat waiting to hear the rest of my father's story. There were so many gaps in my past that I wanted desperately to fill.

"We spoke briefly, but she was certainly not happy to see me. I told myself I would somehow make her fall in love with me again. She didn't even want to talk to me, though. Maggie opened her car door to get inside and I heard something from the backseat. It was the voice of a child. When I looked inside, I saw you. You were just a little thing, but cute as a button." He smiled at me and my heart constricted thinking of the disappointment he must have felt, thinking Mom had moved on.

"Go on," I encouraged.

"When I saw you, I knew right away she was with someone else. It was painfully obvious that the only one still carrying a torch was me. 'You should move on, Will. As you can see,

I have,' was all that Maggie said to me. She got in her car and left, and I didn't follow her. There was no reason to. If she'd shown any inclination that she still loved me, I would have pursued her until she came back to me. But she didn't. She told me to move on. I always wondered about the man who took her away…. So, I started the store. I made a life for myself. It's been good, even if it is a little lonely. There was never any room in my heart for anyone but Maggie. I knew if I couldn't be with her, I wouldn't be with anyone."

"And you never tried talking to her again?" The sadness in his eyes was palpable. I wished with everything in me that my parents' story had ended differently.

"Not really. I saw her around town, but we've never said more than a few words to each other since that day. There were all sorts of rumors about who your father was, but I never asked her. All I knew was that he wasn't in the picture, and I couldn't understand that. The man had you and Maggie, everything I longed for, and he walked away. I often wished I was your father. There was a time when I thought I might be, but that was obviously ridiculous. If that were true, she wouldn't have had any reason to keep it from me." Will shrugged his shoulders.

"What if there's another explanation for everything? Have you ever thought that there might be more to the story?"

"No, I can't say that I have. Honestly, I've done my very best not to think about it at all. I have to say that I've been pretty unsuccessful at that, though." Will smiled sadly and returned to his chair behind the desk.

"But there is more. There's so much more that you don't know." My voice quivered with emotion, and I prayed that I would be able to say what I'd come to.

"What do you mean? What more could there possibly be?"

"Didn't you ever wonder why Mom made such a dramatic change for seemingly no good reason? Didn't you question why she broke up with you when you hadn't done anything wrong?"

"Of course I did! I've questioned it every day since, but the answer is that she didn't love me as much as I loved her."

"You're wrong. Mom loved you more than you could ever imagine."

"She had a funny way of showing it."

"Mom did what she thought she had to for you, for your future."

"You're not making any sense."

"She didn't want you to be tied down to Woodridge. She wanted you to be able to live your dreams. So she set you free."

"Maggie was the only dream I ever cared about. I loved football, but I loved her more. If she'd asked me to choose between the two, I would have chosen her without a second thought."

"Exactly. That's why she didn't give you the choice."

"What do you mean? We could have gone together. Nothing was holding us back."

"That's not true. She was pregnant."

"Pregnant?" Will's eyes flared with hurt and anger. "You mean she was cheating on me while we were together? She was with your father while she was with me?"

"Yes, she was with my father when she was with you, because you're my father." I watched the expression on Will's face change from disbelief, to shock, to pain.

"I'm your father? That can't be true. You must be mistaken."

"No, it's very much the truth. Mom found out she was pregnant, and she knew you would give up your future for her. She knew you would stay in Woodridge and take care of us. She didn't want to tie you down, so she didn't tell you. She didn't even tell me. I just found out myself a few days ago, when I found the letters you wrote her in high school." I stood up, not sure what else to do. I'd said it, and there was no taking it back. The truth was out, and now I just waited for the repercussions.

"I'm your father?" Will stood up from his chair and walked slowly around the desk until he was next to me. He looked at me closely, perhaps seeing for the first time how much we resembled one another.

My heart hammered inside my chest. This was the moment of truth; he would either deny it or accept it. I had no control over either outcome. "Yes, you're my father. Mom told me the truth, and now I'm telling you."

Will looked at me for another minute, and then suddenly he pulled me to him and wrapped his strong arms around me, crushing me in his embrace. His body shook uncontrollably with sobs, and he kept whispering "my daughter" over and over again. I was crying, too, feeling for the first time what a father's embrace was like. He finally pulled away and placed his hands on my shoulders, looking me right in the eyes.

"I'm so sorry. I'm sorry I missed your life. If only I'd tried a little harder to get Maggie to talk to me, this might all have come out years ago. Instead, you grew up thinking your father didn't want you, when nothing was further from the truth."

"I know. I've been angry at my father for years, but knowing it's you, there's not anything to be angry about. Of all the men in the entire world, if I could choose a father, I'd choose you." Tears streamed freely down my face, and I didn't even try to hold them back.

"I've always been proud to know you, but to know that you're my daughter, well, that's just more than I could have ever hoped for."

We wiped our faces and tried to gain some composure. The relief I felt at telling him the truth was overwhelming. I finally felt free, knowing all the secrets were unleashed.

"You're not angry?" I asked tentatively.

"Angry? Maybe I should be, but I'm so happy right now there's no room for anything else."

I hugged him again. Now that I had him, I never wanted to let go. "When I think of all the changes in my life over the last few months, it's kind of mind-boggling. I went twenty-eight years without having a relationship with either of my parents, and now I have you both."

"We have a lot of years to make up for. I know we can't get that time back, but we can start right now and not waste any more."

"You're right. It's time for a new start." I smiled up at my father.

"I need to see Maggie. I need to talk to her, to let her know I understand and that I'm not angry with her. I need her to know that I still love her."

"After all these years? I suppose it shouldn't surprise me so much, but it does. I think it's beautiful. And I think she still loves you."

"That would be too much to wish for. Do you really think it's possible?"

"I do. I think it's more than possible. But be careful with her right now. She's so weak from her treatments, and she's still getting used to the idea of having a relationship with me. What if it's too much for her?" I was very worried about Mom's health and state of mind. I felt extremely protective of her, and while I knew my father's intentions were good, I didn't want to see her upset and overwhelmed.

"If she loves me even half as much as I love her, hearing it will be the very best medicine she could get. I promise I won't hurt her. All I've ever wanted to do is take care of her."

"I'll stay out of it then. This is between the two of you. I should go now. Mom and Kelsey will be home from the hospital soon and I want to be there. I'm sure she's anxious to know how our talk went."

"Thank you, Hope. Thank you for trusting me with the truth. I know this wasn't easy for you. You may not realize it, but you've given me everything I ever wanted, and I'm so proud to be your father." Will hugged me tightly again and said good-bye as I left.

Driving home, I couldn't believe how light I felt. They

said the truth could set you free, and I had to agree. Slowly but surely, I was discovering that emotions weren't meant to be boxed away. They were meant to be felt, even the painful ones.

I did some laundry and housework while I waited for Mom and Kelsey to return. When I heard the car pull into the driveway, I realized I wasn't afraid to tell Mom about my talk with Will. I was happy to finally have it all out in the open.

Kelsey and I settled Mom on the couch, and I brought her a glass of iced water. She was always so thirsty after she got home. Kelsey seemed to know that I needed a few minutes alone with Mom, so she said she was going upstairs to pack. Her stay with me was over, and she had to go home later that afternoon. When we were alone, I turned to Mom and grasped her hand.

"How are you doing?" I wanted to be sure she was up for a conversation before I dove in.

"As well as I can be right now, I suppose. I'm tired, but the nausea hasn't started yet."

"Mom, you know that I talked to Will today." Her eyes widened and I knew she was afraid of what I was about to say. "I told him everything."

"Oh, Hope." Mom sighed deeply. "Even though I knew this day would come, I can't help but be afraid of the repercussions. I'm proud of you for being so brave. I certainly didn't give you an easy situation to deal with, did I?"

"None of that matters anymore. Will… Dad… he was happy.

He was glad when I told him he's my father."

"I'm sure he was. Any man would be proud to have you for a daughter. I imagine he was not too happy with me, though, was he? I'm sure he hates me even more than he did before."

"Not even close. He's not angry with you. He might not be happy with the decision you made, but he understands why."

"That can't be true. He must hate me." Mom shook her head in disbelief.

"It's actually quite the opposite. He still loves you. He never stopped."

"He loves me? That's impossible. You must have misunderstood. Or he's simply being kind. He can't still love me after what I've done."

"But he does. He loves you very much. And I know you still love him."

"Of course I do. I always have." Mom smiled and I caught a glimpse of the happy young girl she must have been all those years ago.

"Maybe it's not too late for you. Wouldn't it be something if you ended up together after all these years?"

"Let's not get ahead of ourselves. In case you haven't noticed, I'm sick. I'm weak. For heaven's sake, Hope, I'm bald!"

"Somehow I don't think any of that is going to matter in the least." I squeezed Mom's hand and stood to go help Kelsey pack.

"I love you. I'm so grateful to be your mother."

"Love you too, Mom." I grabbed a pillow and blanket and helped her make a bed on the couch where I knew she would sleep away the rest of the afternoon. "You can rest now."

Chapter Twenty-Two

Three days later I paced back and forth beside Mom's bed in her hospital room. Things had been going so well, and then last night, she spiked a high fever and I rushed her to the emergency room. Her blood count was off, and she was burning up. She was slipping in and out of consciousness as her body did its best to fight off the germs. With her weakened immune system, it was difficult.

Dr. Riddles warned me months ago that when he lost a patient, it usually wasn't due to the cancer itself. More often, it was because an infection would settle in and the compromised immune system was unable to do its job efficiently.

I glanced at Mom, who lay nearly motionless in the hospital bed. She'd been drifting in and out for the past few hours, and I knew she was in a great deal of pain. I felt desperate, helpless, and very much alone. There was nothing I could do to make things better, no way to fix the situation for her.

I was aware that chemotherapy had risks, but up until now, Mom had been lucky. Yes, she'd lost her hair, fought off nearly constant nausea, and had dropped so much weight she was practically a skeleton. But until last night, she hadn't spiked a significantly high fever, even though I knew it was common. I knew the fever put her very much in the danger zone. She was literally fighting for her life.

I'd spent last night sitting in the chair beside her bed, praying that God wouldn't take her away from me. We'd been robbed of so much time together, and it seemed cruel that she might not make it now that we'd finally found one another.

There was nothing for me to do except wait and pray. Dr. Riddles had told me they could give her medicine to help with the infection, but it was really just a waiting game to see if it would work. So much of it would depend on Mom's will to keep fighting.

"Hope, you should go home and sleep." I was exhausted from the sleepless night, and I'd just dozed off in the chair when I heard her voice.

"You're awake." I leaned over and felt her forehead, a smile breaking out on my face when I realized it was much cooler than it had been earlier. I didn't want to get too excited, but it seemed that her fever was breaking. I pushed the call button for the nurse, who quickly came in and took her temperature, nodding to confirm my suspicions.

"Your fever is going down, Mom. That's great news." I helped her take a sip of her water.

"Did you hear me?" Mom repeated. "I said you should go

home and rest. You're going to get sick yourself."

"That's not going to happen. I'm not about to leave you here alone." I shook my head, determination on my face.

"She won't be alone."

Mom and I both turned toward the doorway. I was shocked when Will walked in the room.

Mom's face, which was already pale, turned the same color as the white sheet that covered her body. She looked desperately toward me, but I was just as surprised to see him there as she was.

"Max." Mom's hands fluttered to her head, self-consciously patting the handkerchief that covered her bald scalp. "You shouldn't be here."

"There's nowhere else on earth that I should be, Maggie." He knelt down beside Mom's hospital bed, and took her small hands into his large ones. My eyes filled with tears, and I knew I was witnessing one of life's rare, pure, beautiful moments.

He continued. "I didn't fight for you all those years ago, but I won't be making that mistake again. I love you, Maggie, and the only way you'll be getting rid of me is if you can look me in the eyes and tell me you don't feel the same way."

"Max, I don't want you to see me… like… this." Mom motioned helplessly at her head and her frail body.

"I've never seen anything more beautiful in all my life."

Mom looked at me and my eyes brimmed with tears as I nodded in encouragement. "Happiness is right there, Mom. Reach out and grab it."

She smiled at me and then turned back to the man she'd loved for years. "Isn't she something, that daughter of ours?"

"She certainly is. I think she must have the very best parts of both of us." The two of them reached out and grabbed my hands, forming a circle. Our family; it was everything I'd ever wanted, but something I thought I'd never have.

"I won't be leaving your mother's side, so you should go home and rest, Hope. That's my first order as your father." He chuckled.

"But what if something goes wrong? I should be here." I'd been glued to her side for months, and I was nervous about leaving her.

"That's part of being a family, honey. No one should have to bear the burden alone." He practically shooed me out of the room as I hugged them both good-bye.

Driving home, I thought of the roller coaster ride I'd been on lately. Just when I thought I'd seen it all, something else happened. Seeing my parents together was surreal, but the love they had for one another was so obvious. I didn't know what was ahead for them, but I was glad that all their skeletons were finally out of the closet. Wading through the pool of secrets that constructed my life was an exhausting venture, and I hoped I'd finally reached the other side.

It was amazing to see how unconditionally my parents still loved one another after all these years. After all the obstacles life had thrown in their path, they had somehow found their way back to each other. Few people had a love that was strong enough to overcome all the things they had. I used to believe that Sam and I had that kind of love, but these days I wasn't sure.

I had avoided him since Kelsey and I'd had dinner at his house. He'd called me several times, but I never answered. Taking a chance and starting over was a hard thing to do. I'd done it with Mom and was attempting to do it with my dad. It was difficult, but somehow I'd managed. With Sam, the fear went even deeper, and I honestly didn't know if I could let myself be that vulnerable again. After the fallout because of Annie's pregnancy, I understood that I was the one who had destroyed our future together. What I didn't understand was why Sam had run to Annie that night. If he loved me, how could he sleep with her? Maybe I had no claim to him at that point, but it still hurt that he'd slept with her. Although I accepted responsibility for what I'd done to him, I wasn't sure if I was brave enough to give our love a second chance.

The truth of the matter was that I'd single-handedly destroyed my world, and I'd never forgiven myself for it. If I were honest, I knew Sam had suffered too, possibly even more than I had. After all, both of our decisions set into motion the domino effect that ultimately made him a father. Bridget and Sam were a packaged deal, and as much as I loved him, my love for his daughter made it impossible to just walk away. It also made the stakes much higher.

For a large portion of my life, I'd blamed Sam for my unhappiness. I blamed him because I couldn't love Jonathan. I blamed him for the fact that he had a child and I'd lost mine. I blamed him for years and years of loneliness, when in fact, those things were never his fault. I was the one in charge of my life, not Sam. The choices I'd made were because of me, not him.

For too long, I had placed my entire life's happiness and disappointment in the hands of a teenage boy. Of course, now I knew that was ridiculous. No one was responsible for my happiness except me. With sudden clarity, I understood that it was time to finally let it all go. I still loved Sam, and he'd made it clear that he still loved me. The only person standing between me and the future I wanted was me, and it had been that way all along.

Mom and Dad were getting their happy ending, and maybe it wasn't too late for me and Sam. I would go to him and tell him I wanted a second chance. I would fight for my future instead of allowing it to slip through my fingers once again. Resolve settled in. I wouldn't wait a moment longer.

I pulled into the driveway and noticed an unfamiliar car. I wondered who it could be, but no one was inside of it. I quickly parked my car and got out, feeling uneasy. Anger bubbled inside as a familiar figure walked around the side of the house.

"Jonathan. What are you doing here?" I didn't even try to disguise the animosity in my voice.

"That's no way to greet me, is it? I missed you, Hope. I brought you something." Jonathan placed a small box in my hands, but I didn't open it.

"You're delusional. You're not welcome here." I shoved the box back at him, refusing to hold it a second longer. I knew it would be another expensive gift, probably jewelry from the size and shape of the box. He seemed to think he could buy my forgiveness, but he couldn't have been more wrong.

"You won't answer my calls. You ignore my texts. You even returned the gifts I sent you. So I flew out here to see you. What was I supposed to do?"

"You're supposed to leave me alone. That's what divorced people do, Jonathan."

"But we're not divorced yet."

"We would be if you'd just sign the papers!" I raised my voice as anger and rage spilled out. "You did this. You had an affair, not me. I miscarried our child because of the stress you put on me."

"Don't be so self-righteous, Hope. We both know that I may have been the one who had an affair, but you were unfaithful to me in your heart from the day we met." He spat the words at me, and I took a step back.

I'd never seen him so angry in all the years I'd known him. His face grew redder by the second, and his hands were balled up in fists at his sides. I backed away and he pursued. Feeling the car behind me, I knew I was cornered. There was nowhere for me to go, and I was actually afraid of him.

"You need to calm down. Traveling across the country to yell at me isn't going to change my mind. We are finished." I stood my ground, even though I was starting to panic.

"We will never be over!" He raised his voice even more. He was yelling so loudly that I knew he could probably be heard down the street.

Glancing past him, I saw Sam approaching. Things were about to go from bad to worse. I looked helplessly at Sam, warning him with my eyes to go away, but he continued walking toward us.

"What seems to be the problem here?" His voice startled Jonathan, who backed away from me and turned around to face him. The two men stood in the driveway, sizing each other up.

"There's no problem. You should go back home and mind your own business." Jonathan sneered at Sam, even though he had no idea who he was. He'd never met Sam; he'd only ever heard about him.

"Well now, you've made it my business by yelling so loudly that all the neighbors can hear. So I'll ask you again, what seems to be the problem?" Sam was angry, and I saw him clench and unclench his jaw.

"I don't have a problem. This is between me and my wife." Jonathan glanced back at me with a look of smug satisfaction on his face, as if he'd just cemented the fact that I belonged to him.

"Your wife?" Sam looked at me and his face transformed from angry to hurt. I knew what he must think. He had no idea I was married, and in that moment, I had no way of explaining the real story to him.

"Yes, my wife. Now if you'll excuse us." Jonathan turned his back on Sam and faced me again.

"Hope, is this true? Is this man your husband?" Sam spoke quietly. I didn't answer for a minute. I wasn't sure what to say. After all, Jonathan was legally still my husband.

"Sam, you don't understand. We're getting—" I started to explain, but he turned away from me. Without another word, he walked briskly back home, went inside, and slammed the door so loudly the sound reverberated through the neighborhood.

Now I was angry. *How dare Jonathan come here and cause a scene!* It was time to put an end to this insanity once and for all.

"It's time for you to leave, Jonathan. You and I are over. We should never have been together to begin with. You know it as well as I do. I don't love you. *I do not love you.* I never did. I know it's not what you want to hear, but I cannot say it any more clearly than that. Sign the papers. Go away, and stay out of my life!" My voice trembled as I yelled louder than I ever had before. He was still standing in front of me and I pushed him away from me. I stumbled as I walked away from him, and he reached out to steady me, but I shook his hand off me. "Do not touch me. Ever again."

I'd never spoken to Jonathan like that, but he'd never given me any reason to do so until then. I was shocked at his behavior today. In all the years I'd known him, I'd never been afraid of him, and I was through being afraid of life.

Shame washed over Jonathan's face, and I knew I'd finally gotten through to him. He backed away from me and walked to his car. Only minutes before, his face had been contorted in anger; now he just looked sad. Before getting inside he looked at me. "I'm sorry I came here today. I'm sorry I yelled at you. I just… love you, Hope. I always have. And I messed it all up."

"This isn't completely your fault. I know I never gave you what you needed, and I'll be the first to admit it. We just weren't right for each other from the beginning. But we had a lot of good years, and we were always friends. You were there for me when I needed someone, and you helped me grow up.

Let's just leave it at that, okay? Let's part on good terms, knowing that we served a purpose in each other's lives, but that purpose is over." I spoke the words that were in my heart, knowing that they were true.

"Hope… I… okay. I'll sign the papers as soon as I get back. Just promise me one thing?" Jonathan's eyes met mine.

"What?"

"Promise me that you will hunt down the ghost that's haunted you all these years. Find Sam. He's very much a part of you. Find him and tell him you love him. It doesn't even matter if he doesn't feel the same way anymore. You'll never be free until you do. Good-bye, Hope." With that, he got into his car and drove away. I knew it was the last time I'd ever see him.

Jonathan's words played over and over in my mind as I stood in the driveway. *Find Sam. Tell him you love him. You'll never be free until you do.* He'd never spoken words that were truer, and I finally understood. Without a second's hesitation, I ran next door and banged loudly on Sam's front door. He opened it, but he didn't look at all happy to see me. I knew I had to explain about my marriage.

"What do you need, Hope? Does your *husband* know you're here?"

"If you'll just let me explain, Sam—"

"I'm sorry, but I need to get Bridget from school and take her shopping for some new shoes. She's grown out of everything she has. I really don't have time for this conversation right now. If you'll excuse me…." Sam pushed the door shut, but I threw out my hand to stop it.

"Sam, just listen to me."

"No, Hope, I don't think I will. You know, I've always thought we belonged together. For me, there's never really been anyone but you. I can see that wasn't the case for you. You should go now, before your husband comes looking for you." He closed the door without another word, but the devastation on his face was obvious.

I walked back home, my heart a heavy lump inside my chest. I was beginning to believe that Sam and I might never be together. Life just kept throwing one obstacle after another between us. Just when I thought nothing was in our way, another hurdle appeared that we had to jump over, and I was tired of jumping. Maybe it was time to just accept the fact that no matter how much we loved each other, we weren't meant to end up together. Maybe fate was telling me to wake up and move on with my life.

Chapter Twenty-Three

The next morning my eyes popped open as the tantalizing smell of bacon frying and coffee brewing wafted into my bedroom. My first thought was that I must be dreaming, but when I realized I wasn't, I sat up with a start. When I had gone to sleep last night, I was alone in the house. From the smell of things downstairs, I wasn't alone anymore.

Mom was still in the hospital, so who was downstairs cooking? After silently panicking for a moment, I grabbed my robe and walked quietly down the stairs, glancing into the kitchen as I reached the bottom. I brought my hairbrush along, just in case I needed a makeshift weapon, although I was aware that most intruders didn't cook breakfast. Luckily, it wasn't necessary. I breathed a sigh of relief when I saw that it was my father, although I was definitely confused about why he was cooking in our kitchen.

"Good morning." He turned around and smiled when he heard me walk in. "I hope I didn't scare you."

He had, but I certainly wasn't going to admit it. "Good morning. Did I forget we'd arranged to have breakfast this morning?"

"No, you didn't forget anything. Your mom gave me the key and suggested I come over and see you. She's doing well, by the way. Dr. Riddles says she'll be home by tomorrow."

"Tomorrow? That's amazing. What a relief!" My father showing up at the hospital had certainly given Mom the strength she needed to keep fighting. I was grateful to him for giving her what I couldn't. "I'm so glad you've been there with her. It's good for her, you know. Having you back in her life is just what she needed."

"It's good for me, too." He smiled as he dished up eggs and bacon onto two plates, offering one to me as we sat down at the table across from each other.

"This looks delicious. What did I do to deserve you cooking breakfast for me this morning?" I still felt a bit awkward around him, but I knew that time would remedy that. I couldn't be happier to know that this kind, generous man was my dad.

"You're my daughter. That's reason enough. You know, no matter how many times I say it, it still surprises me." He chuckled softly as he shook his head and began to eat.

"I know the feeling. I went through so much of my life alone. These days, it seems I'm never alone. I think having so many people who love me will take some getting used to." It was all a bit overwhelming, all these new relationships in my life.

"Your mom thought it would be a good idea for us to

have some time alone, to talk."

"Did you want to talk about anything specific?" I shoveled a forkful of eggs into my mouth, curious about the real reason he was here this morning. I knew there was more to it than cooking breakfast for me.

"As a matter of fact, yes. I have something important to ask you. But first, there's something I need to show you."

"Okay, what is it?" I was definitely curious now.

He went into the kitchen and picked up a large box I hadn't noticed before. He carried it into the dining room and placed it on the floor in front of me.

"Open it," he prompted.

I gently lifted the lid, and inside the box were piles of letters. I looked questioningly at my father, but he simply nodded, motioning for me to open one. I lifted the first one out of the box and slowly opened the envelope with trembling fingers. Somehow, even though I had no idea what the letters contained, I knew they were important. I began reading. It was a letter written to my mother, dated five years after I was born.

In the letter, my father wrote about his life. He shared stories; common, everyday things that weren't of any real importance. He talked about the salmon he caught that day, what he planned to eat for dinner, and the fact that it had been a busy day at the store. It concluded with him telling my mother how much he loved her.

Curiously, I reached inside and grabbed another letter. It was very similar to the first, but was dated two years after the previous one. I began grabbing letters quickly, opening them, inspecting the dates, and skimming the written words. They were all some variation of the same thing. There was nothing groundbreaking; no earth-shattering information was found on the pages. It was just my father's thoughts on an ordinary day in time. I didn't understand.

"What is this?"

"You said you read the letters I sent to your mother when we were in high school, and I thought maybe you would want to see the rest of them."

"The rest of them?"

"Yes, Hope. I started out writing a letter to your mother each year on the anniversary of the day we met. Even after our relationship ended, I never stopped loving her. Since I couldn't tell her, I had to do something. So I wrote her letters, then I put them in this box. If you count them all, you'll find much more than twenty-nine, even though that's how many anniversaries there have been. You see, there was so much I wanted to tell her that I would often write more than one a year. Some years were especially hard, so you'll find one written nearly every day."

I couldn't believe what I was seeing. My father loved my mother so much that he'd continued communicating with her even after they were no longer together. The topic on which he wrote was never important; he just wanted to share his life with her in the only way he knew how. I wondered if he'd shown Mom these letters yet. The depth of their love continued to amaze me.

My father cleared his throat. "Now I have something to ask you."

"What's that?" I had a feeling I knew the question even before he asked it.

"How would you feel if your mother and I got married?" His voice quivered with nervousness, and I thought it was the sweetest thing I'd ever heard.

"I would feel like it's long past due." I smiled at my dad, who appeared relieved at my answer.

"Oh, thank goodness." He exhaled loudly. "I was hoping that's what you'd say!"

I cleared my throat, nervous about what I needed to say. "Now, I have something to ask you."

"Ask me anything. I'm an open book."

"Well, my whole life I've known you as Will. Now that I know the truth, calling you that just doesn't feel right. Would you mind if I called you Dad?" I swallowed hard.

His eyes brimmed with tears. "I would be honored. I don't think there's anything I'd like to hear more."

I stood up and hugged him, the whole situation feeling a bit surreal to me. I knew this was yet another life-altering event that would take some getting used to.

"When's the big day, Dad?" I tested out the word, which felt a bit foreign on my tongue. I knew with time I would get used to it.

"Well, I wanted to do it tomorrow, but your mother shot that idea down right away. It can't happen soon enough for me. I've wanted to be Maggie's husband since I was a kid." Dad rattled on, talking quickly and animatedly about his upcoming nuptials. He certainly didn't have cold feet about getting married. "But your mother wants to wait until she's stronger and feeling more like herself, so that's what we'll do."

"Whenever it happens, you both have my blessing and all of my love." I squeezed his hand, so amazed at the little twists and turns of life.

We ate the rest of our breakfast while Dad chatted on and on about the wedding plans. When we finished, we cleaned up the mess and washed the dishes. We straightened up the rest of the house together too, knowing Mom would be home tomorrow and would expect to find it spotless. It was nice to have his help. Being able to count on another human being was something to which I was still adjusting, but it was a nice idea to get used to.

"I'm going to head back to the hospital. Your Mom will be wondering how our little talk went. She was a little bit nervous about telling you, I think." Dad smiled sheepishly, and it was easy for me to picture the young man he once was.

"Well, you can assure her that I couldn't be happier. Let her know I'll swing by tonight and see her." I hugged him good-bye and he returned to the hospital.

My parents were getting married. What a strange idea! As a romance author, I made a living writing about the concept that true love conquers all, but it was an entirely different thing to see it played out in real life with my own parents. Perhaps there was some truth to the idea that two people who were meant to be together couldn't be kept apart. Maybe real love didn't only live inside the pages of a romance novel.

That thought always brought me back to Sam. As a naïve girl, I'd believed that he was my true love. Even after everything that happened, a small part of me still held on to that belief. In spite of my pain and fear, I wanted the fairy-tale ending with him. But with all the problems we kept encountering, I honestly didn't know if it would ever happen.

One thing was certain—I knew I still needed to explain my situation with Jonathan. He needed to hear the truth. If nothing else came of it, I wanted Sam to know I loved him. He was probably upset that I hadn't told him I was married sooner. Granted, I should have. Right before we kissed in his kitchen would have been the ideal time, but I had other things on my mind then. Now, I knew I had to find a way to convince him to hear me out; he needed to know that very soon Jonathan wouldn't be my husband anymore. *Find Sam. Tell him you love him. You'll never be free until you do.* Jonathan's parting words echoed again in my brain.

I walked next door, determined to talk to him before I lost my nerve. I knew if I waited, I would back out. Instead of Sam answering the door, though, it was June. My heart sank.

"June, hello." I hadn't seen her in weeks, and I'd missed her. But for the first time since I'd met her, I felt awkward. My guilty conscience gnawed at me because of the horrible thoughts I'd had toward her daughter. Learning that Annie had died in childbirth completely changed my perspective.

"Hello, Hope. Please come in." June motioned for me to enter, but I hesitated, momentarily losing my nerve to talk to Sam. "I'm the only one who's here at the moment, if that's what you're worried about. Bridget is at her friend's house, and Sam is out on the boat."

June always had a sixth sense when it came to saying the

right thing to me. I appreciated her kindness, and I'd come to cherish her friendship. I didn't want there to be any difficulty between us, no matter what had transpired between Sam and me.

"All right, thanks for inviting me in." I followed her into the kitchen, and took the seat she offered at the table.

"Would you like some tea? I've found that when you're a bit unsettled, there's nothing like a cup of tea to set things right." She smiled at me, but didn't wait for my answer. She was already filling the teakettle. I nodded and she joined me at the table while the water heated.

"You know, this misunderstanding between you and Sam has gone on long enough. You need to find a way to fix it." June went straight to the heart of the matter, and I was a bit surprised that she knew about Sam and me. I hadn't ever confided in her that we were involved, and I couldn't imagine that he had talked to his almost mother-in-law about his feelings for me. Maybe Annie had told her the story at some point.

"I've tried, but it seems like one thing after another always happens. You don't understand. It's like fate is determined to keep us apart." I shrugged in frustration.

"Nothing can keep two people apart if they really belong together, Hope. And I just might understand more than you know." She patted my hand in her calming way. "Sometimes in life you have to fight the hardest for the things that mean the most."

"You know, I can't believe you're trying to help Sam and me get together. After all, Annie was your daughter. I know you must have loved her very much. I don't understand why you would want him with me."

"Hope, I love Sam like he's my own son. He's a good man, and a fantastic father. Why do I want you two together? Because he deserves happiness, and so does my granddaughter. You would make them both very happy. Why wouldn't I want that?" June placed her hand over mine and looked me directly in the eyes. I was shocked when I saw nothing there but sincerity.

"I know you have a kind heart, June, but it must bother you to think of Sam with someone else. I don't think you know the whole story."

"I know all of it, every last sordid detail. I know things about my daughter that no mother should ever have to know. But I've learned to come to terms with it all, in time." June had a faraway look, and I wondered if she was picturing her daughter.

She took a deep breath and continued speaking. "Annie was a wild girl. I knew that better than anyone. When she told me she was pregnant, I honestly wasn't surprised. I did my best with her, but she had a mind of her own from the beginning. I was glad to learn that Sam was the father, though. When I met him, I knew right away that he was a good boy, and I knew he would someday grow into a good man. I was right about that."

"Yes, there's no one else like him." I spoke quietly.

"Right before Annie went into labor she told me the whole story, the real story. She said that she'd made a terrible mistake and wanted to fix it. She broke down in tears and confided in me that the night she and Sam were together, well, this is hard for a mother to say about her daughter…." She stopped and appeared to be wrestling with whether or not she should continue.

"Go on, June, please go on." I grabbed her hand.

"After you and Sam fought at the beach that night, he went into town. Annie said she and her friend came up with a plan to make you angry with him in the hopes that you would break up with him. Apparently, it worked. Annie followed him to the grocery store, and she said that his eyes were red and swollen. She said she could tell that he'd been crying. As you well know, Annie had had a crush on Sam for years, and she saw this as her big chance. She asked him if he wanted to talk about it, and he was so upset that he said yes. Maybe he thought if he could get another girl's perspective on the argument he would have a better chance to win you back. I don't know his reason for going with her that night."

My stomach tightened with nervousness. I'd never heard this story before, and I'd always wondered exactly what happened. "What then?"

"Well, somehow Annie got her hands on some alcohol that night and they went to the beach together. Long story short, they got drunk and Annie took advantage of that fact. I'm not saying that he didn't know what he was doing, but I do believe he wasn't in his right mind when he did it. A few weeks later, she found out she was pregnant. I think you know the rest." June finished her story with a sigh.

My mind reeled with all the new information it was

attempting to process. Since that horrible night, I'd envisioned every possible scenario of what might have happened between Sam and Annie. I'd pictured each sordid image in my mind over and over again; I'd tortured myself with the thoughts. But in my wildest imagination, I never thought of this one. Sam had been drunk, or at the very least, impaired, when he slept with Annie.

If he was upset enough to confide in Annie after our fight, he was probably distraught enough to drink with her. It didn't change the fact that they slept together, but somehow it made the situation easier for me to take. It was a relief in some ways to know that he didn't make a sober, conscious decision, which was what I'd always believed.

"I didn't know any of that. I imagined it all quite differently, to be honest." I began to understand that nothing seemed to be the way I thought it was.

"I'm aware that you didn't know. I've always believed that the only reason Annie told me the truth when she went into labor was that she knew she wasn't going to make it through." June looked me in the eye as she spoke the next words. "I think she understood that she was going to die, Hope. And she wanted to do the right thing, finally."

June's words chilled me to the bone. Had Annie known that she was going to die giving birth to Bridget? It seemed a bit far-fetched, but stranger things have happened. "That's a lot to take in."

"Yes, I know it is. But there's more, and this is the part I really want you to hear."

I swallowed nervously, wondering what revelations could

possibly be left.

June continued. "Right before she died, Annie made me promise that I would find a way to get you and Sam back together. She knew how much Sam loved you, and she also knew she'd acted underhandedly to get what she wanted. She hoped to make amends somehow. I promised her I'd try, but I didn't even know who you were back then. I only learned about you when Sam and Bridget moved back here and I met your mother. When you came back to Woodridge, I knew that was my chance to honor my daughter's wishes. I didn't know how I was going to go about it, but then you and Bridget took to each other right away. It all fell into place without me lifting a finger."

I couldn't believe what I was hearing. The Annie I knew never thought of anyone other than herself. Why would she care if Sam and I were happy? Had pregnancy really changed her that much?

"June, are you telling me that Annie's dying wish was that Sam and I would end up together? That seems a bit melodramatic, don't you think?"

"That's exactly what I'm telling you, Hope. You can call it whatever you want to. Annie told me that Bridget needed a mother, and the only person she wanted in that role was you. She said Bridget was the child you and Sam might have had together, and she was sorry she got in the way of that. She wanted you to be Bridget's mother if she couldn't be." June was crying now and my heart went out to her. It must have been so difficult for her to dredge up all those painful memories about her daughter.

"I don't know what to say. I don't know what to do, June." I was crying myself at that point, and grabbed a napkin off the table to wipe the tears away.

"I know exactly what you need to do. You and Sam belong together. You know it, he knows it, and Annie knew it. I think Bridget knew it too, from the first time she met you. It's up to you to make it happen. Remember, when two people are meant to be together, nothing on earth can keep them apart. Find Sam. Tell him you love him." June's words mirrored Jonathan's, and I realized I needed to listen to them.

"You're right. It all makes sense to me now." I jumped up from the chair, and wrapped my arms around her. "I need to find Sam. Where is he?"

"He went out on the boat early this morning. He should be coming in to port soon." She gripped my hand tightly in hers. "Go to him, Hope. Help me make Annie's wish come true."

"I will. Thank you."

Chapter Twenty-Four

I ran home and grabbed my purse and car keys, jumped into my car, and drove as fast as the speed limit would allow toward the port. I parked the car and walked quickly toward the docks, pushing down the nervousness. My entire future rested on what was about to happen, and I just hoped Sam would give me a chance again.

I had no idea which boat was his. I glanced up and down the marina, hoping to catch sight of him, but I soon discovered that to my untrained eyes the boats all looked very similar. After several minutes of searching, I still hadn't found him.

It didn't matter; I wasn't going to give up that easily. I spotted a fisherman working on a boat further down the docks. He looked up from his work when I approached.

"Excuse me. I'm looking for Sam Mooney. Do you know him?" I prayed silently that the man could help me.

"Sure, I know Sam. He usually comes in about this time. He'll dock right over there." The man pointed to the right of where we were standing, just a few spaces over. "He shouldn't be much longer if you want to wait on him."

"Thank you." I ran down the dock to the spot where the man had pointed. Looking out in the distance, I saw a large boat heading toward the shore. I assumed that must be him.

I watched the boat grow closer, and as it did, my heart began to beat faster. I'd waited ten years for this moment, and now that it was here, I was scared to death. There was so much at stake; not only my happiness, but Sam's and Bridget's as well. All our futures hung in the balance, and I knew that whatever we said today would make or break that future.

The vessel grew larger as it sailed closer. Finally, I was able to make out the figure of the man standing on deck, and I knew without a doubt it was Sam. His shaggy blond hair blew in the breeze, and his strong, sturdy body looked like it was an extension of the boat itself. He worked quickly, moving back and forth across the deck, his confidence apparent in every single step. He was truly in his element on the water. I marveled at the man he'd become.

When I'd left Woodridge ten years ago, he'd been just a boy; a scared boy who was trying to make the very best of an impossible situation. Not many teenage boys would have had the decency to stick around and be a father. Sam's character wouldn't let him do anything else, and while I should have admired him for it, I hadn't ever been able to see beyond my own pain. I'd blamed him for years because he hurt me. Selfishly, I'd never even tried to think of what he must have gone through. As I looked at the man he'd become, I felt a surge of pride. I didn't know how much I truly loved him until that very moment.

Sam expertly maneuvered the vessel into the open space in front of me. For the first time, I noticed the name of his boat. I sucked in my breath as I read the words painted in large, bold letters across the stern, *Always Hope*. I blinked away tears as I digested the fact that he had named his boat after me.

When the vessel came to a halt, I knew what I had to do. It was now or never. He hadn't yet spotted me, so I took a deep breath, wiped my sweaty palms on my jeans, and walked toward him. I stood directly in front of his boat and cleared my throat so he would notice me. Sam looked up from his work, and his blue eyes locked on to mine. His face registered surprise, but then quickly turned to irritation. It wasn't exactly the welcome I'd expected, but I wouldn't let it deter me.

"What are you doing here, Hope?" He didn't sound angry, but he did sound frustrated. I knew he didn't want to see me.

"We need to talk." I left little room in my statement for an argument.

Whether he wanted to talk to me or not, he was going to. I wasn't giving up this time. I'd spent my whole life running, but now I was determined to stand my ground and fight for what I wanted, and I wanted him more than I'd ever wanted anything. He was worth fighting for.

"There's nothing for us to talk about." He busied himself with the ropes, refusing to meet my eyes.

"That's where you're wrong. We have a lot to talk about.

More than you could ever imagine. So either you're coming down here, or I'm coming up there." Honestly, I hoped he decided to come down to the docks. I had no desire to fall overboard trying to get onto his boat.

"I'm busy, but I'll give you five minutes." He glanced at his watch and then back at me.

"I'm afraid I'm going to need more of your time than that, but it's a good start." I smiled timidly, hoping to chisel my way past the wall he'd built against me.

He sighed and reluctantly climbed off the boat and joined me on the dock; he shoved his hands into his pockets and stared at me. The pained look on his face nearly killed me. I kept reminding myself that he was worth whatever I had to do to get him back. I motioned him toward a nearby bench, and he followed. I sat down on one end and he sat on the other. It felt like there were miles between us, and I wondered if I could really bridge the distance. So many things, both spoken and unspoken, lingered between us.

"What do you have to say?" Sam spoke quietly. "Does your husband know you're here?"

"That's what I want to explain. You have the wrong idea about Jonathan. He is my ex-husband. The paperwork is finalized."

"Ex-husband? Does he know that? He seemed pretty possessive of you when I saw him in the driveway that day." He looked at me uncertainly.

"That was his last-ditch effort to get me back. I think he knew deep down that wasn't going to happen, but he wasn't ready to give up yet. He went back to New York and signed the papers a few days later, and that's the end of it."

"I didn't even know you were married, Hope. Can you imagine what that felt like? Thinking of you being married to someone else?" Sam raked his hands through his hair, but stopped quickly as he realized the irony of what he'd just said.

"Yes, I can imagine. That's what I've lived with for ten years, imagining you married to someone else. It was the worst thing I've ever felt." I met his eyes and saw the deep pools of pain. I'm certain he saw the same thing in mine.

"Why did you get divorced?" His face looked agonizingly sad, and I knew far too well how difficult it was to fight past all the pain we had caused each other. I had finally done it, and I hoped he could too. "Do you still love him?" He looked at me expectantly, and I knew our entire future hinged upon my answer to that one simple question.

"No, I don't. The truth is I never really did. I tried to, but I couldn't."

"Why?"

"Because my heart belongs to you, it always has."

"Why did you marry him if you didn't love him?"

"I've asked myself that question a million times. The only answer I can come up with is that I was running away. I was trying to escape. I believed you and Annie got married, so all I wanted to do was get out of this town, and go as far away as I could from all the hurt. Jonathan offered that opportunity, and I took it. I ran from you, from my mom, my dad, and all the other painful memories here in Woodridge."

I swallowed hard before continuing. "I kept running for

ten years. If Mom hadn't gotten sick, I would probably still be running. I told myself every single day if I kept going, eventually I'd outrun the memories. But I never did."

His face softened and he moved closer to me.

"Hope—" He started to say something but I interrupted him.

"Please, just let me get this out before I lose my nerve." He nodded and I continued. "It all comes down to this. I love you. I've loved you since I was fourteen years old. And no matter what you say today, I'll love you until the day I die. And I finally realize that none of the rest of it matters. I love you, without conditions, and without expectations. I just… love you."

He rose and stood with his back to me, facing the water. I knew he was replaying every word I'd just said in his mind, trying to determine if we were worth the fight. I knew that's what he was doing, because it's exactly what I'd done the past few weeks. After a few minutes of painful silence, he returned to the bench and sat right next to me. My heart pounded rapidly as our eyes met.

"I've waited so long to hear you say those words. You're all I've ever wanted." He cupped my face in his hands and our lips met in a kiss that was filled with promise. In that moment, I felt the final fragments of my heart slide gently into place.

I returned his kiss with more passion than I'd ever felt in my life. Finally, after all these years, he was mine and I was his. I pulled him closer to me, feeling like I would never get enough of him. He stood, lifting me off my feet and into his arms. I knew there were other people at the marina, but I didn't even care.

"I want you more than I've ever wanted anything before." My voice sounded breathless.

"You have me. You have me forever. You're never getting rid of me again." He began walking, still carrying me in his arms.

I looked around, suddenly aware that we were being watched by the fishermen in the boats nearby. "We have an audience."

He gave me the mischievous look that I remembered and loved so much and planted another smoldering kiss on my lips. It's a good thing he was carrying me, because his kisses always left me weak in the knees.

"Looks like you found some treasure, Sam," the weathered fisherman in the boat next to us called out.

"Sure did, Joe. I found the best treasure of all, and I'm claiming her for my own," he replied as he lifted me over the edge of his boat before climbing on board himself.

"Enjoy!" Joe chuckled as he climbed off his boat and retreated down the dock.

"What are we doing?" I had no idea what he planned, but I was up for it, as long as we were together.

He wrapped his arms around me and kissed me again. "I thought you might like to see the cabin."

"The cabin? What's in there?" I smiled teasingly.

"You'll see." He took my hand and led me through the door of the small space. There wasn't much to look at in there, but I went along with it anyway.

He punched some buttons into the keypad and opened

up a safe in the wall of the boat. He took out a small, black box. I knew what was inside before he even opened it. My eyes began to fill with tears as he dropped to one knee. He reached inside the box and took out a beautiful, glistening, oval-shaped diamond ring. Taking my left hand in his, he kissed it tenderly.

"Hope, I've carried this ring around with me for a very long time. I bought it years ago, long after you'd left town, knowing I might never get to give it to you. The past couple of weeks I've contemplated throwing it overboard, but I'm sure glad I didn't." He smiled and I could tell he was nervous. He continued. "I've wanted to ask you this question since I was fourteen years old. Will you marry me?"

My heart was bursting with happiness. Tears spilled from my eyes as I said, "Yes, I'll marry you, Sam. A thousand times, yes!"

He slipped the lovely diamond onto my finger, and I practically jumped into his arms when he stood. Finally, after all this time, we were getting our happy ending.

"I love you. I love you so much."

"I'll love you forever, Hope. It's you and me against the world, just like I always said." As he spoke those words, our words, he pulled me next to him. I rested my head on his chest and felt with certainty that after all these years I'd finally found my home.

As we stood on the *Always Hope*, I knew that I was where I belonged. I'd come back to Woodridge lost and adrift, aimlessly floating in a sea of bitterness and pain. Slowly and excruciatingly, I'd navigated through the waves of heartache.

I had worked hard to finally get to this place, and I was confident that my anchor was firmly set.

They say you can never really go home again, but that wasn't exactly true. I had come back to Woodridge, but what I had found was a different home; a home that hadn't even existed before. I discovered a new depth to my love for Sam, appreciation and understanding for my parents, and gratefulness for finding Bridget and June. But what I had really found was myself, and that was the compass that finally pointed me to my true north.

Epilogue

Six Months Later

I watched proudly as Bridget scattered the rainbow-colored petals down the white aisle runner. Woodridge Community Church was positively bursting with gerbera daisies. I had to agree with my mother's assessment all those years ago that they were indeed the happiest flowers. When we planned this day, we wanted that happiness to be felt by all who joined us. Looking around at the smiling faces of all the people I loved, I marveled once again at the winding road that had led me to this moment.

Taking a deep breath, I clasped Mom's trembling hand in mine. The look we exchanged spoke volumes as we took the first step and started down the aisle together. We were both dressed in lovely ivory wedding gowns, a luxury we hadn't forgone when planning this double wedding. Mom didn't want to put a lot of money into a dress, but I insisted. This was her wedding, and she deserved to walk down the aisle to my father in a dress she loved.

I had surprised her with a beautiful, vintage, ivory lace sheath dress that was my gift to her. The stunning dress hugged her body, which was finally beginning to fill out now that her chemotherapy treatments were over and she'd been declared cancer free. That was the best and most important gift of all. Her lovely auburn hair was beginning to cover her head once again, although it was still short. She carried a bouquet of gerbera daisies, and tucked inside the bouquet was the very first letter my father ever wrote to her.

I'd also chosen a dress I loved. It was made of flowing ivory chiffon, and its empire waist was specifically designed to disguise my five-month baby bump. Thankfully, I was past the morning sickness, and my doctor assured me that this pregnancy was moving along exactly as it should be. I'd been so worried that I would never conceive again, but that hadn't been a problem at all. Every day I was learning that life was all about perfect timing.

Sam and I had been quietly married in a ceremony at City Hall six months ago, just a week after he proposed at the marina. After being apart for ten years, neither of us wanted to wait a moment longer. Having a double wedding meant so much to Mom that we agreed to go along with it, even if it was just a formality. I loved the symbolic significance of the ceremony. It was the perfect conclusion to the second-chance love stories we both shared.

Mom and I reached the end of the aisle, and I leaned over and kissed her cheek, brushing away the tears that glistened there, before placing her hand into my father's. Once their hands were joined, I brought them both to my lips and planted a kiss there as well. These two people had given me life, and although it hadn't always been an easy one, for better or for worse they were mine. I turned and put both of my hands into Sam's, knowing I'd already placed my future there.

The minister cleared his throat and began, "First Corinthians chapter thirteen tells us, Love is patient, love is kind. It does not envy, it does not boast, it is not proud. It does not dishonor others, it is not self-seeking, it is not easily angered, it keeps no record of wrongs. Love does not delight in evil but rejoices with the truth. It always protects, always trusts, always hopes, and always perseveres. And now these three remain: faith, hope and love. But the greatest of these is love." I listened to the words I'd specifically chosen for the minister to speak. I let them sink in as I thought about the journey I'd been on this past year.

Sam and I were finally living the life we'd always planned, even though it wasn't exactly the way we'd envisioned it. In many ways, it was so much better than anything our teenage selves could have concocted. It wasn't the starry-eyed, reckless kind of love we used to share. Instead, it was mature, tried, true, and something neither of us would ever take for granted. It was exactly the kind of love that we needed.

I'd legally adopted Bridget, who was once and for all my daughter in every sense of the word. I thanked Annie each and every day for giving her to me. She was a precious gift, and I was blessed to be her mother. She filled my heart with happiness, and I had become the mother she'd always needed. Soon, Sam and I would welcome another child into our family.

Sometimes, I still fell into my old habits. The familiar anxiety was hard to bury, and I often found myself waiting for disaster to strike, certain that this was all too good to be true. I would think that I must be dreaming, and I would be terrified that I'd awaken to find none of this was real. Day by day, though, I believed it a little bit more. This was my reality, and I planned to hold on to it for dear life.

Sam looked at me and smiled knowingly as my eyes filled with tears. I'd told him before the ceremony that I wasn't going to cry, and he laughed as if I'd just said the most ridiculous thing in the world. He was right; he knew I couldn't make it through this momentous day without tears. He knew me better than anyone. I smiled at Kelsey, who was sitting in the front row with her husband and children, and she winked slyly at me. She'd known that this was my future long before I had.

I glanced at Mom and Dad, and my heart nearly burst with love for the two of them as they gazed into one another's eyes. After a lifetime of separation, they had found their way back to each other, proving that it was never too late for a happy ending.

Mom caught me looking her way and our eyes locked. We'd certainly walked along a rocky path to find our way to each other, but we were so close now that I couldn't imagine my life without her. It was strange to think that if she hadn't gotten sick, none of this would have happened. Now she was in remission, and our future was bright. Life certainly had a way of giving us exactly what we needed when we least expected it.

Although my return to Woodridge began as a desperate attempt to escape my life, it turned out to be a gift I could never have imagined. In the process, I gained a mother and a father, as well as a husband and a daughter. But most importantly, I found myself, and I knew I would never lose me again.

The minister's words echoed in my head: "Now these three remain: faith, hope, and love." I'd been haunted throughout my life with many things I'd never wanted—fear, anxiety, depression, loneliness, and abandonment. A year ago, I thought they would remain with me forever. Bit by bit, they were replaced with other things, like happiness, acceptance, and peace. The pain of the past was finally gone. Love was all that remained.

The End

Acknowledgements

Heidi would like to acknowledge her extended family, both near and far, as well as her Hot Tree Publishing family, who have welcomed her aboard with open arms.

About the Author

Heidi Renee Mason is a passionate romance novelist and crafter of your next happily ever after. She loves listening to the voices in her head (from her characters, of course!) and creating worlds in which her readers can lose themselves for a little while. A native of the Midwest, Heidi now resides in the Pacific Northwest with her husband and three daughters.

Connect with Heidi:

WWW.FACEBOOK.COM/HeidiReneeMason
WWW.HEIDIRENEEMASON.WORDPRESS.COM

About the Publisher

Hot Tree Publishing opened its doors in 2015 with an aspiration to bring quality fiction to the world of readers. With the initial focus on romance and a wide spread of romance sub-genres, we envision opening up to alternative genres in the near future.

Firmly seated in the industry as a leading editing provider to independent authors and small publishing houses, Hot Tree Publishing is the sister company to Hot Tree Editing, founded in 2012. Having established in-house editing and promotions, plus having a well-respected market presence, Hot Tree Publishing endeavors to be a leader in bringing quality stories to the world of readers.

Interested in discovering more amazing reads brought to you by Hot Tree Publishing or perhaps you're interested in submitting a manuscript and joining the HTPubs family? Either way, head over to the website for information:

/WWW.HOTTREEPUBLISHING.COM

www.ingramcontent.com/pod-product-compliance
Lightning Source LLC
Chambersburg PA
CBHW050513190726
48284CB00003B/792

* 9 7 8 1 9 2 5 4 4 8 5 6 6 *